SWORN

BOUND BY BLOOD BOOK 3

ALSO BY RICHARD FIERCE

DRAGON RIDERS OF OSNEN

Trial by Sorcery
A Bond of Flame
The Warrior's Call
The Coin of Souls
Wings of Terror
Eyes of Stone
Tooth and Claw
The Servant of Souls
Smoke and Shadow
The Dark Rider
The Song of Bones
Sword and Crown
Tides of Darkness
Wrath and Ruin
Tomb of Oaths

MARKED BY THE DRAGON

Curse of the Dragon
Scale of the Dragon
Egg of the Dragon
Call of the Dragon
Wrath of the Dragon
Sacrifice of the Dragon

SWORN

BOUND BY BLOOD BOOK 3

RICHARD FIERCE

Sworn

Copyright © 2024 by Richard Fierce

Cover design by Christian Bentulan

Dragonfire Press

Print ISBN: 979-8-89631-046-4

SHAOING
SHINRAHA MOUNTAINS
TATENAGAWA
IKJE
DANGJU
ZHENCHENG
WONCHEOK
JINSEONG
TAEPO
KIMCHON
GANGCHEOK
POSONG
LEGEND
CAPITAL
SHRINE
CITY
MOUNTAINS

CHAPTER 1

Akuhara stood atop a cliff overlooking the Drakka encampment, her dark armor glinting in the light of hundreds of campfires scattered across the valley below. The air was thick with the scent of smoke, and she wrinkled her nose at the smell. Her dragon lay coiled beside her as she gazed out at the horde with a mixture of pride and unease.

The encampment was a chaotic sprawl of tents, sharpened stakes, and roving Drakka. Their guttural growls and hissing filled the air, a discordant symphony that grated against Akuhara's thoughts. She could see them moving in restless clusters, sharpening weapons, devouring raw meat, and occasionally snapping at one another. They were powerful, yes, but undisciplined, unruly.

Her magic was the only thing keeping them in line.

She inhaled deeply, the weight of this war pressing down on her.

What do you suppose they think of me? she wondered, her gaze lingering on a pair of Drakka snarling over a scrap of meat.

They fear you, her dragon rumbled, its voice a low growl that resonated in her mind like thunder. *As they should.*

Akuhara's lips twisted into a bitter smile. *Fear is a powerful tool. It keeps them obedient. But it's not enough.*

The dragon tilted its head, smoke curling from its nostrils. Its eyes narrowed as it studied her. *Doubt lingers in your heart. Why?*

Akuhara's hand clenched into a fist. Her nails bit into her palm, the pain grounding her. *Because this wasn't how it was supposed to be. I wanted to rebuild, to create something better. But these... creatures... they only understand destruction.*

Her words hung in the air, and the dragon's gaze didn't waver. *Destruction is the path to rebirth,* it said finally, its tone edged with impatience. *To create something better, you must first sweep away what is broken.*

Akuhara turned away, her jaw tight. Her gaze drifted to the horizon, where the flickering lights of a distant city dotted the landscape like fireflies in the night. The sight stirred something deep within her—a memory, unbidden and unwelcome.

The air in the gardens had always smelled of jasmine and freshly turned soil, a heady mix that still lingered in Akuhara's mind even now. She had been no more than eight, crouched behind a cluster of towering azaleas, her knees pressed into the damp earth as she peered through the gaps in the leaves. Ahead, a girl stood in the sunlight, a wooden training sword gripped tightly in her hands.

The girl—Kai—moved with unpolished determination, swinging the sword in wide arcs. Her brow furrowed in concentration, and sweat glistened on her forehead as her breath came in quick, sharp bursts. Beside her, an imposing man stood with his arms crossed, his expression stern yet proud as he corrected her stance.

"Again," he commanded, his deep voice carrying across the garden.

Kai nodded and adjusted her grip, her small frame trembling with effort. She was so focused, so utterly absorbed in the task, that she didn't notice Akuhara watching. No one did.

Akuhara remained hidden, pressing herself further into the shadows of the azaleas. She wasn't supposed to be there. She wasn't supposed to exist. Left behind at birth, presumed dead, she had been swept away into the embrace of the Drakka. And yet, drawn by curiosity or some unnameable force, she had found her way back here, to this garden, to this girl who shared her face.

As Kai completed another swing, the man stepped forward, placing a hand on her shoulder. "Good. But strength alone isn't enough. You must learn to anticipate, to see what comes next."

Kai looked up at him, her eyes wide with determination. "I will. I'll make you proud."

Akuhara's chest tightened. Pride. Approval. These were things she had never known, raised as she was among creatures who valued only destruction. Watching this moment felt like gazing into a life that could have been hers, a life stolen from her the moment she was cast aside.

Her nails dug into the damp earth. She wanted to step out from her hiding place, to confront the man, the girl. To demand answers. But what would she say? That she was the daughter they abandoned? The child they never knew?

She turned away, her small hands curling into fists. Even at that age, the bitterness had already begun to take root, twisting through her like the tendrils of dark magic she would one day wield. But alongside it was something else, something softer. A yearning to be seen, to be acknowledged, even if only from the shadows.

"One day," she whispered to herself, the words barely audible. "One day, they'll know."

The memory faded as quickly as it had come, leaving Akuhara standing on the cliff once more, the scent of jasmine replaced by smoke and ash. She closed her eyes, exhaling a slow, measured breath.

Perhaps, she said, her tone softer now, tinged with a weariness she couldn't entirely suppress. *But sometimes, I can't help but wonder...*

Her dragon shifted beside her, its massive form blocking out the campfires below. *Your sister is a weakness,* it hissed, the venom in its tone unmistakable. *She clings to a broken world. You are stronger without her.*

Akuhara didn't respond immediately. Instead, she knelt and placed her hand on the earth. The ground beneath her palm was cold, unyielding. Tendrils of dark energy seeped from her fingertips, snaking into the soil like roots of a malignant tree. The Drakka nearest to her stiffened, their eyes sharpening into focus as her magic strengthened their bond. She felt their fear, their hunger, their rage— all of it feeding into her power, bolstering her control.

They follow because they fear, Akuhara said, her eyes fixed on the writhing energy beneath her hand. *But fear can turn to defiance. We must act soon before the tide shifts.*

The dragon loomed closer, its massive head lowering to her level. Wisps of smoke drifted from its nostrils, and its eyes burned like embers. *Then give the order,* it rumbled. *Let the cities burn. Let their hope turn to ash.*

Akuhara stood, her expression hardening. She raised her hand, the dark energy crackling around her. *No more waiting,* she said. *We march at dawn.*

CHAPTER 2

The sky burned crimson, streaked with black smoke that blotted out the stars. Kai stood in the center of the battlefield, her hands trembling as she gripped her sword. Around her, the ground was littered with the fallen, their faces obscured by ash. The stench of blood and charred flesh choked the air, but it was the silence that pressed down on her like a vice. Not a single cry or groan of pain, only the crackle of distant flames and the low rumble of something vast moving in the shadows.

"Hikari?" Kai called, her voice hoarse and small against the oppressive stillness. She turned, searching for the gleam of her dragon's gold scales.

A shadow shifted, and she froze. Emerging from the smoke was Akuhara, her twin sister, clad in dark armor that shimmered with magic like oil on water. Her dragon loomed behind her, its eyes glowing a sickly green, its scales blackened and twisted as if burned from the inside.

Akuhara smiled, a cruel twist of her lips. "Did you really think you could stop me, sister?"

Kai raised her sword, but her hands shook. "I won't let you destroy everything."

"Oh, Kai," Akuhara said, her voice dripping with mockery. "You already have." She gestured around them, and Kai's heart dropped as she saw the faces of the dead. Ryn, Master Satoshi, the Sundered—all staring at her with lifeless eyes, blame etched into their features.

"No," Kai whispered, taking a step back. "This isn't real."

Akuhara laughed, a chilling sound that echoed across the battlefield.

The ground trembled as Hikari emerged from the smoke, but something was wrong. Her scales were streaked with veins of black, her eyes clouded with the same sickly green light as Akuhara's dragon.

"Hikari?" Kai's voice cracked. She reached out a hand, but the dragon snarled, baring fangs that dripped with venom.

"She's mine now," Akuhara said, stepping closer. "You were never strong enough to be her rider."

Hikari reared back, her massive wings casting Kai in shadow. Then, with a deafening roar, the dragon lunged.

Kai screamed as darkness swallowed her.

She jolted awake, her breath coming in ragged gasps. Her hands clawed at the dragon skin cloak she had wrapped around herself, the Heart of Flame pulsing faintly at her side. For a moment, she didn't recognize her surroundings—a campfire's dim glow, the quiet rustle of trees. Hikari lay a short distance away, her scales gleaming softly in the moonlight as she slept.

Kai pressed a trembling hand to her chest, willing her racing heart to calm. It was just a dream. A nightmare. But the fear lingered, curling in her gut like a living thing.

Hikari stirred, her eyes opening to meet Kai's. *What's wrong?* the dragon asked, her voice a low rumble in Kai's mind.

Kai shook her head, unable to find her voice. She glanced at the sword lying beside her, echoes of the nightmare flashing in her mind.

It's nothing, she said finally, though the words felt hollow. *Just... a dream.*

Hikari tilted her head, her gaze piercing. *Dreams often reveal truths we try to ignore.*

Kai swallowed hard, the image of Hikari's twisted form still vivid in her mind. She looked away, staring into the dying embers of the fire.

We should get moving, she said, her thoughts steadier now. *Akuhara's out there, and I... I won't let that dream become reality.*

Hikari huffed softly, a plume of smoke curling from her nostrils. *Then let us ensure it does not.*

Kai nodded. The nightmare had shaken her, but it had also ignited something deeper—a determination to face her sister, no matter the cost.

She crawled over to the fire, brushing her fingers through the dirt to extinguish the last of the embers. The faint crackle died away, leaving only the chirp of crickets and the occasional rustle of leaves in the night. She stood, slinging the dragon skin cloak over her shoulders, its weight and warmth a reassuring presence against the chill of the night air.

Hikari rose to her feet, stretching her wings wide. The moonlight caught on her scales, and for a moment, Kai found solace in the sight.

We continue East, Kai said. *To Ikje.*

Hikari lowered herself, allowing Kai to climb onto her back. The familiar feel of the dragon's scales beneath her hands comforted her, pushing away the tendrils of the nightmare that tried to claw at her mind. With a mighty beat of her wings, Hikari launched into the air, the ground falling away beneath them. The wind rushed past Kai's face, cold and carrying the scent of pine.

As they soared higher, the stars came into view. Their distant glow would soon vanish, as dawn was nearing.

Kai tightened her grip on Hikari's neck, her gaze fixed on the horizon. They flew for a while in silence until Kai spotted a small village, its wooden houses clustered together. No smoke rose from chimneys, and the silence was unnatural, thick and stifling.

Something feels wrong, Kai said, her right hand instinctively going to the hilt of her sword. She patted Hikari's neck. *Take us down.*

The dragon rumbled in agreement and descended. Her claws kicked up dust as she landed at the edge of the village. Kai slid from Hikari's back, her boots crunching against the dirt. The air was still—too still. Even the usual chirping of crickets was absent.

Kai scanned the empty streets, then cautiously stepped toward the nearest house, its door hanging ajar. Inside, overturned furniture and shattered pottery told a story of sudden violence.

The faint scent of blood reached her nose, metallic and sharp. Her stomach turned, but she pressed forward, her blade drawn. Outside, Hikari's low growl drew Kai's attention to the shadows beyond the village square. Movement. A flicker of light reflected off dark, scaled bodies.

"Drakka!" she shouted as the creatures burst from their hiding places.

The first Drakka lunged, its claws slashing through the air. Kai sidestepped and swung her blade in a clean arc, slicing through its neck. The creature's lifeless body crumpled to the ground, but more took its place, their guttural snarls filling the silence.

The Drakka moved with eerie coordination, flanking Kai as they pressed her toward the square. She parried one strike, her sword clanging against the creature's talons, then ducked another swipe aimed at her head. A third Drakka lunged from her left, and she barely twisted out of its reach.

Hikari roared, unleashing a torrent of flame that lit up the square. The fire scattered the Drakka, some of them shrieking as their scales blackened and cracked. They regrouped quickly, swarming from alleys and rooftops. Kai's mind raced. There were too many of them.

Hikari, the ridge! she called, pointing to a narrow ledge above the village. If she could collapse it, it would crush the Drakka below.

Hikari launched into the air, her wings beating powerfully. Kai darted between attackers, slashing and parrying as she made her way to higher ground. The Drakka pursued, their talons gouging the earth as they climbed after her. She reached a crumbling staircase carved into the cliffside, her legs burning as she sprinted upward. Below, the Drakka surged forward, their eyes fixed on her.

From above, Hikari dropped a boulder onto the ridge. The rock groaned and splintered, cracks spiderwebbing across its surface. Kai pressed herself against the cliff wall as a thunderous crash echoed through the valley. Tons of rock tumbled down, crushing the Drakka in a cloud of dust and debris.

Breathing heavily, Kai looked down at the devastation. The ground was littered with broken bodies and shattered stones. Hikari landed beside her.

We need to keep moving, Kai said, wiping blood from her sword. *There could be more.*

As they took to the skies, Kai cast one last glance at the ruined village. She spotted movement among the rubble—one Drakka, barely alive, dragging itself from beneath the rocks. Its eyes met hers for a brief moment before Hikari's shadow enveloped it, and Kai turned away.

They flew in silence, the ambush weighing on her. *They're getting more intentional,* Kai finally said. *That didn't feel random.*

No, Hikari agreed. *Someone is watching us.*

Kai's thoughts darkened. Akuhara. Her sister's shadow loomed over every move the Drakka made, every life they destroyed. She clenched her jaw.

She will pay for all of her crimes.

CHAPTER 3

Ikje had fallen.

Kai's stomach lurched as Hikari circled over the scorched ruin. The once-impenetrable city had been reduced to rubble, its stone walls toppled and its streets abandoned. Charred remains of houses stood like skeletal sentinels, their wooden beams cracked and blackened. The place resembled that of a graveyard more than a city.

We're too late, Kai said, feeling her throat constrict.

A part of her had hoped, naively perhaps, that Ikje would somehow survive the onslaught. As she took in the collapsed towers and the vast emptiness where markets had been, she realized that hope was a fragile thing.

Take us lower, she bade Hikari.

The dragon banked sharply, her wings cutting through the air as they descended toward the city. As they approached, the stench of ash and death grew stronger. Kai swallowed hard. She had never seen such destruction, but it was more than that. This... this was personal. Her parents had been here. Had they managed to escape, or had she lost them as she had lost Liu and Kokoro?

Hikari landed softly amid the wreckage of what had been the main square where the Ceremony of Oaths had taken place. Kai slid from the dragon's back and landed on the cobblestones with a thud, her boots stirring up clouds of soot. Her eyes flicked over the debris. All around her, the silence was oppressive. There were no signs of survivors, but Kai decided to search anyway.

"Hello? Is anyone here?"

She wandered among the ruins and stopped near a half-destroyed fountain. The water was long gone, replaced by dust and ash. In its center, the stone figure of a dragon still stood, though its face was cracked and broken.

Kai continued to pick her way through the ruins. She may not have been able to prevent this tragedy, but she would do everything in her power to ensure it never happened again. Her cloak flapped in the wind as she walked, darker than the blackened stones beneath her feet.

A sudden movement caught her eye. Her head snapped up, and she caught a glimpse of a figure walking among the rubble. Without hesitation, she sprinted ahead, Hikari following close behind.

"Wait!" Kai called.

The figure turned, and Kai's breath caught in her throat. It was an elderly woman, her face streaked with soot. She clutched a rag to her face, and her eyes widened with terror at the sight of Hikari.

Kai lifted her hands in a gesture of peace. "We're not here to hurt you."

The woman hesitated, her gaze darting between Kai and Hikari. "The Drakka," she rasped. "They did this."

"I know. Is there anyone else here?"

The woman shook her head. "Those who survived went to Dangju."

Kai remembered Master Satoshi commanding the Sworn to flee there during the attack, but it didn't make sense for everyone to go there. Zhencheng was closer.

"We can take you to Dangju. Do you have family there?"

"My family is gone," the woman replied. "They died here fighting the Drakka."

"I'm sorry." Kai felt helpless, and she looked at Hikari. "We can take you somewhere else, somewhere safe."

"This place is safe. The Drakka have already destroyed it. I doubt they will come back. Leave me be, child, and do what you must."

"Can you tell me where Dangju is?"

"Go east. It's on the coast."

The woman walked away, and Kai sighed. She could force the woman to come with them, but she didn't feel that was the right thing to do. She watched the woman until she disappeared behind the remnants of a building, then she turned to Hikari.

We need to stop Akuhara before she destroys another city, but we can't do it alone. We need the other Sworn.

The dragon rumbled her agreement. *We can leave now, but what of the Sundered? They'll be here soon.*

We'll backtrack and let them know to continue on to Dangju. It'll take them longer than us to get there, but they can catch up.

Hikari lowered herself to the ground and Kai climbed up her shoulder. With a powerful thrust of her wings, the dragon launched into the air. The ruins of Ikje spread out beneath them like a grim tapestry of destruction. Kai leaned forward, her fingers gripping Hikari's scales as they soared west. They didn't have to fly far before the Sundered came into view.

There, Kai said, pointing. *They're making good time.*

Hikari descended, landing far ahead of them so she didn't scare their horses. Kai remained on the dragon's back, waiting for the Sundered to draw nearer. Ryn was leading the group, and he dismounted, handing the reins to one of the others.

"What's wrong?" he asked as he approached.

"Ikje is gone," Kai answered. "We're going to Dangju instead."

"Gone? How? Its walls have never been breached before."

"I know. With Akuhara leading them, the Drakka have become an organized force. It seems nothing can stop them." Kai paused, unsure how Ryn would react to her next words. "Master Satoshi and some of the other Sworn are in Dangju. I know you don't care for the empire, but we're stronger together."

Ryn stared at her in silence. Finally, he nodded. "I can't guarantee the others will come, but I swore an oath of loyalty to you. I will go where you go."

"You willingly gave that oath. I did not request it, nor will I require you to fulfill it. But I would be grateful if you fight alongside the Sworn with me. The same goes for the others." She nodded toward the Sundered who waited behind him.

"We fight as one for the sake of our fallen dragons," Ryn said. "We will meet you in Dangju."

"Thank you. I will see you in a few days, then. May your travels be safe."

Ryn bowed his head and returned to his horse. Hikari took to the air again, flying east this time. The wind whipped through Kai's hair, and for a moment, she forgot about the world below and reveled in the feeling of flight.

Hours passed, marked only by the gradual movement of the sun across the sky. Kai's muscles ached from the prolonged flight, but she refused to complain. Instead, she focused on the changing landscape below, using it to distract herself from the fatigue.

I've never seen this part of the empire before, she told Hikari.

Do you see that formation of rocks?

Kai peered down, spotting an unusual circular arrangement of boulders. *What is it?*

An old nesting ground. Long abandoned, but once home to my kind.

Dragons in general, or elders?

Elders.

Kai stared at the place in awe, but a hint of sadness overtook her for the loss of the elders. Hikari was the last one. What did that mean? Would something happen to the world at Hikari's passing? She was hopeful that day wouldn't come for many years, but the thoughts plagued her regardless.

Over the course of the next two days, the landscape gradually transformed. Tall mountains and lush forests gave way to rocky cliffs, and the distant shimmer of the coast appeared on the horizon. A gust of wind slammed into them, nearly unseating Kai. She pressed herself close to Hikari's neck and held on tighter.

The coastal winds are strong, but we survived a storm. This is nothing!

Hikari roared and beat her wings harder, fighting against the turbulent air. The gusts came sporadically, making a steady flight impossible. They pressed onward, leaving the cliffs behind and finding sprawling hills that eventually flattened to grassy plains. In the distance, Kai could see smoke, but it was too faint to be from an attack.

I think that's Dangju, Kai said.

The city came into view, and the first thing Kai noticed was the city's defenses were more robust than Ikje's. The walls stood high, lined with ballistae, and from her vantage point, she could make out rows of soldiers moving about in formations.

Beyond the city, the blue waters of the Bay of Five Winds lapped against the shore. Boats were docked at the nearby harbor, and the smoke she had seen earlier rose from chimneys scattered throughout the city. The air was thick with the scent of salt and fish, and she felt Hikari's stomach rumble with hunger.

A horn blared, and Kai scanned the city walls to see several ballistae turn and take aim at them. Kai straightened and waved one arm in the air.

Hold on, Hikari said.

Kai's eyes widened as the soldiers launched several bolts. They whizzed past them, barely missing their mark.

Land, quickly! she urged.

Hikari dipped her wings and dove toward the ground. Kai hoped their arrival wouldn't face any further hostility if they landed outside of the city. They touched down near the gates, and a host of Sworn flew over the walls, surrounding them.

"Stay your weapons," a familiar voice shouted. "It's Kai Lin."

CHAPTER 4

The cavernous nest deep beneath the earth pulsed with life. The walls of the chamber shimmered faintly, streaked with glowing veins of molten energy, and the air was thick with the heat and dampness of the underground. At the edges of the room, clusters of Drakka eggs lay nestled in shallow pits, their translucent shells glowing faintly with the promise of life. The sound of their faint, rhythmic pulsations mingled with the guttural growls of the generals who surrounded Akuhara.

She stood at the center of the chamber, a crude stone table before her. Her dragon stood behind her, its molten eyes glowing in the dimness. Akuhara raised her hands, summoning a swirl of dark energy that coalesced into a flickering map of the empire. Mountain ranges and rivers glimmered faintly, marked by the strategic locations she had chosen. The Drakka generals leaned forward, their eyes fixed on the projection.

"Xeroth, Kalrek," Akuhara growled in their guttural tongue, her voice filled with authority. The two largest Drakka stepped forward, their hulking forms towering over her. "Your forces will divide."

She pointed to the glowing map, tracing a path toward Dangju. "Xeroth, you will take half of the army southeast. Burn Dangju to the ground. Leave no survivors." The Drakka rumbled in approval. "Once the city demolished, you will meet us here."

Her hand shifted to Zhencheng, the imperial capital, where the lights of the empire still burned defiantly. "Kalrek, the other half marches with you and me to Zhencheng. We will crush their heart and extinguish their hope."

The generals snarled in excitement, their guttural cries reverberating through the cavern. Akuhara's dragon mirrored their satisfaction. She projected confidence, but beneath her commanding exterior, unease gnawed at Akuhara's resolve.

The resistance they had faced was stronger than she had anticipated. She couldn't shake the feeling that these attacks would only serve to unite the empire, not break it apart. Splitting her forces was risky, but she would shield the Drakka that traveled to the imperial city with her magic, hiding them from prying eyes until it was too late for the emperor to stop them.

As the generals left to ready their forces, Akuhara lingered in the cavern. She stared at the flickering map, her fingers brushing against the glowing outline of Zhencheng. She knew she was walking a dangerous path, but with each passing day, her grip on power tightened, and the whispers of fear that followed her name grew louder.

But there was one person whose voice still rang clear in her mind: her sister. She couldn't forget the look of triumph in Kai's eyes during their last battle. Akuhara couldn't help but feel a sense of dread at the thought of facing her again.

Her dragon spoke, shattering her thoughts. *The Drakka hunger for blood. You cannot control them forever.*

"I know," Akuhara whispered aloud. She closed her eyes, exhaling slowly. *Once the empire is ash, their purpose will end. And so will they.*

The dragon's eyes glowed brighter, its voice laced with curiosity. *You would destroy them? Your own kin?*

Akuhara turned to face the beast, her expression hard. *They are not my kin. They are a means to an end.*

The dragon hissed but said nothing more. Akuhara turned back to the map. She had no illusions about the Drakka's nature. They were creatures of chaos, incapable of building the world she envisioned. But the thought of what must come after filled her with dread.

Her voice was a whisper as she stared at the flickering map. "The empire deserves to fall, but I will not trade one tyranny for another. When the time comes, I will find a way to end the Drakka."

The dragon growled softly behind her, its presence a constant reminder of the storm she had unleashed. Akuhara's gaze remained fixed on the map, her resolve hardening like steel. There was no turning back now. To rebuild, she would have to destroy everything—including the monsters that had taken her in.

CHAPTER 5

Relief washed over Kai as she stared at Siran. It had only been a few weeks since they had parted ways, but the woman looked as different as Kai felt inwardly. She glanced at the other Sworn and saw Jiro, Ichiro, Kazu, and the others from Ikje. She nodded to each of them and turned back to Siran.

"The guards seem on edge," she said.

"They are. A Drakka army is heading this way as we speak. Our scouts are tracking their movements."

"I didn't see anything on the way here. Which direction are they coming from?"

"The north. They'll be here by nightfall." Siran looked from Kai to Hikari. "This isn't the dragon from the ceremony."

"No, she isn't. This is Hikari."

31

Siran bowed her head to the dragon. "Master Satoshi will want to see you. He sent a message to Tatenagawa but never received a reply. We feared the worst."

"I'm fine, but..." Kai clenched her jaw. "Things will only get worse if we don't stop the Drakka once and for all."

"Come," Siran said. "I will take you to Master Satoshi."

Siran and the other Sworn took to the air and flew over the wall. Hikari followed them, and Kai looked down at the city. It was a sprawling metropolis, with shops and markets bustling with people. Soldiers manned the watchtowers, keeping a vigilant watch over the landscape. If she didn't know any better, Kai would have no idea the city was preparing for an assault.

They landed outside a massive complex that served as the barracks. Kai swung a leg over Hikari's side and dropped to the ground.

"Your dragon can find food and water here," Siran said. "She can also rest in any of the open stables."

I'll be back soon, Kai told Hikari, running a hand along the dragon's neck. Hikari nuzzled her in return, and Kai fell into step beside Siran. The streets were crowded with both soldiers and civilians, but Siran parted the throng with authority.

"Are you in charge of the Sworn?" Kai asked.

Siran looked at her questioningly. Her expression shifted from confusion to a smile. "No, I am not. I would like to lead one day, assuming we survive."

Kai returned the smile, but she didn't like Siran's dark words. They had to survive. They were the empire's only defense.

"They've fortified the city well," Kai said. "But it will take more than walls to hold back the Drakka."

"We've been preparing while also training. It hasn't been easy, and most of the others still aren't ready, but we've run out of time. They are moving more quickly than we expected."

"That's because they have a leader now."

"What do you mean?"

"You know, don't you? The woman who took my dragon at the ceremony is behind all of this."

"Your twin sister?"

"Yes. She is aligned with the Drakka and leads them. That's why they are more organized now."

They approached a grand structure with towering columns and intricate carvings that blended the empire's martial heritage with artistic elegance. The heavy doors swung open as they neared, and Siran took the lead, guiding Kai through the hallways to a large chamber where a group of people were gathered around a circular table.

Master Satoshi looked up, meeting Kai's gaze. She bowed her head to him and said, "We need to talk."

He immediately dismissed his council, Siran included. Once the room was cleared, the two stood in silence for a long moment before Master Satoshi spoke.

"You are different. Your *ki* radiates strength, and I sense a powerful aura of magic. Tell me everything."

Kai obeyed, relaying everything that had happened to her since she'd originally left Ikje. Master Satoshi frowned briefly when she mentioned bonding with Hikari, but otherwise, he listened intently without speaking. When she pulled the Heart of Flame out of her silk bag, its pulsing light cast an otherworldly glow across the room. She held it up for him to see, and her cloak billowed of its own accord.

"The legends are true," Master Satoshi said, his expression grave. His eyes, usually sharp and discerning, now held a mix of awe and deep-seated worry.

"I did not think such artifacts were real. The power you wield is beyond anything I've encountered in all my years. Your bond... it is both a gift and a curse."

"What do you mean?"

"Power always comes at a price, Kai. And bonding with an elder dragon..." He trailed off, shaking his head. "It is forbidden for a reason. This gemstone and cloak, too, carry their own dangers. Together, they make you a formidable force, but also a target."

Kai's brow furrowed. "A target? For whom?"

"For those who fear power they cannot control," Master Satoshi replied grimly. "The emperor himself would view this as a threat to his authority."

The weight of his words crashed down upon her. Her chest tightened, and she swallowed hard before asking, "What would happen if the emperor found out?"

Master Satoshi lowered his voice despite there being no one else in the chamber. "It means certain death, not just for you and your dragon, but for any who know of your bond."

Deep down, Kai knew the answer before he confirmed it. She clenched her hands into fists to keep them from shaking. "But I am fighting *for* the empire. Eradicating the Drakka is my sole concern. I never meant to put anyone in danger. My bond with Hikari... it feels right, as if it was meant to be. How can something so powerful, so pure, be wrong?"

"The emperor won't see it that way. He will see you as a threat, and he will act accordingly. That is why he can never know."

"What?" Kai's eyes widened in surprise.

"We must keep it a secret, no matter the cost," Master Satoshi replied.

Kai took a deep breath and met his intense gaze. She couldn't believe he was vowing to deceive the emperor. He barely knew her, and yet he was willing to risk his position, and even his life, for her.

"Thank you, Master. If I can help prevent more bloodshed, then I'm willing to face whatever consequences may come. Please do not risk your life for me. If the emperor finds out, tell him you didn't know."

"Your courage is commendable. Have you told anyone else?"

"No. Liu was the only one, and..." Kai trailed off, and Master Satoshi took her hand in his.

"Liu was a great warrior. He died protecting you, as was his duty. His sacrifice will not be forgotten."

Kai knew his words were sincere, and she nodded. "Siran said there is an army of Drakka headed here. What can I do to help?"

"Fight, when the time comes. We have done everything we can to prepare. Now, we wait."

CHAPTER 6

As night fell, the glow of torches illuminated the city. Kai stood at the top of one of the many watchtowers, her eyes turned upward to the vast expanse of stars overhead. The cool night air was a welcome reprieve from the heat, and she heaved a sigh.

"Do you think it will be enough?" she asked, looking at Siran. Kai had volunteered to keep watch with her, mainly because she couldn't sleep. Her nerves were too on edge, and the anticipation of what was to come kept her mind racing.

"It has to be," Siran replied. "If we fall—"

"We won't," Kai interrupted. "We can't. I just meant... I don't know. I hope we're ready."

"Readiness is a luxury rarely afforded in times of war, but we are as ready as we can be." They were silent for a moment before Siran continued. "Forgive me. I don't mean for my words to sound so dark. I have seen more death than I care to, and there will be more to come before it is all over. It weighs heavily on me."

"I understand."

Kai turned her gaze to the sky again, tracing the familiar constellations. The Hunter, The Dragon, The Imperial Crown. They glowed clearly in the heavens, constant and unchanging despite the chaos that brewed far below them.

The sound of thunder drew Kai's attention to the north. It hadn't looked like it would rain earlier, but she quickly realized it wasn't a storm approaching. A dark mass appeared on the horizon, growing larger with each passing moment.

Siran scrambled to her feet and alerted the city by ringing the enormous bell atop the tower. The noise echoed into the night, and the other watchtowers soon joined in the warning. Kai watched as the mass drew steadily closer, the endless ranks of Drakka causing the very ground to tremble.

They are here, Kai told Hikari. *I'm coming to you.*

She raced down the stairs of the tower, sprinting through the empty streets to the barracks. Hikari was already out of the stable, and she lowered herself to the ground so Kai could climb onto her back.

"Sworn, to your mounts!" Master Satoshi's voice rang out.

In a flurry of motion, riders took to the sky, circling above the city. Kai and Hikari joined them, watching as the first wave of Drakka crashed against the walls like a tidal wave. The creatures clawed their way up the stonework, but they were met with sword and spear as the soldiers on the parapets hacked and stabbed at them.

Kai could feel the tension in Hikari's body, a coiled spring waiting for the right moment to strike. Kai patted the dragon's neck.

Wait for the signal, she said.

The air filled with the sounds of battle. Clanging metal, screams, and the roars of Drakka intertwined into a cacophony of noise.

Kai's heart pounded in her chest as she watched the conflict unfold. The soldiers fought bravely, but the sheer number of Drakka threatened to overwhelm them.

"Defend the walls!"

She barely heard Master Satoshi's command over the wind, and Hikari was flying toward the wall before Kai realized what was happening. She drew her blade and held on tightly as the dragon dove down sharply, pulling up at the last second to latch her rear claws onto the top of the battlements.

A flap of her wings sent a gust of wind into the nearest Drakka, and they went tumbling backward. Hikari opened her jaws and unleashed a torrent of flames. The fire lit up the night, and Kai's eyes widened. The Drakka's numbers were beyond counting. The acrid smell of burning flesh in her nostrils broke her reverie, and she glanced along the wall.

Archers loosed volleys of arrows, and the other soldiers fought with everything they had. She caught sight of a few faces. Their eyes were wide with fear, but they fought on, knowing the cost of failure. A Drakka scaled the wall, climbing over the top and attacking a young soldier.

Without thinking, Kai leaped from Hikari's back and slashed the creature across its back with her sword. The Drakka howled in pain and fury as it recoiled, giving the soldier time to regain his wits and launch his own attack. Together, they backed the creature against the wall, where Hikari promptly swatted it into the air. Its roar faded among the noise, and the soldier offered Kai a grateful nod before returning to the wall and slashing at more Drakka.

There is something out there, Hikari said.

What is it?

I'm not sure. It feels like a dragon, but it's... different.

Kai looked out at the sea of Drakka, but nothing stood out. Then she heard it. A deep, resonating roar that vibrated the air around her. In the distance, a shadowy form emerged. It towered over the Drakka, larger and more sinister than anything she'd seen before. Its eyes burned with malevolence, and Kai was overwhelmed with terror.

She stood frozen in place, unable to tear her gaze away from the dragon-like beast. Its scales were black as midnight and seemed to swallow the surrounding light. The soldiers around her faltered, their movements slowing as they caught sight of the colossal beast. Kai's fear was pushed away by a fierce determination that flooded the bond.

We must stop it, Hikari said. *There is no one here strong enough but us.*

Kai wasn't so sure about that, but the dragon's confidence bolstered her spirit. She nodded and climbed back onto the dragon's back. A horn blared behind her, and Kai looked over her shoulder to see the Sworn gathering into a formation.

They're going to try to attack it, Kai said.

Then we need to strike first.

Hikari leaped into the air and sailed over the army of Drakka, flying directly toward the monstrous beast. As they drew nearer, Kai pulled the Heart of Flame out of her bag and gripped it tightly. It pulsed in her hand, radiating a warmth that spread through her arm and into her chest.

The creature locked its fiery red eyes on them as they approached, seeming to recognize the threat they posed. It reared back, spreading its enormous wings, and roared again as it took to the air. The sound crashed over Kai, thick and heavy, like the weight of death itself. Hikari flinched, and Kai could feel a ripple of uncertainty in their bond.

Hikari banked to the side, dodging a sudden burst of dark liquid the creature spewed from its maw. It struck the ground below, burning through the Drakka horde and stone alike, leaving the ground scorched and sizzling.

In response, Hikari breathed her fire, sending a stream of flames hurtling toward the beast. The blaze met its dark scales, but to Kai's horror, they barely left a mark, flickering out as if snuffed by an invisible wind. Hikari whipped around to avoid a retaliatory swipe of its talons, and Kai's stomach lurched.

This creature was no ordinary dragon; it was something darker, something twisted by magic. They couldn't simply burn it—they needed a strategy.

We need to lead it away from the city, Kai said. *It'll give us time to find a weakness.*

Hikari rumbled in agreement and flew south, baiting the beast to follow. With a furious roar, it trailed after them like a shadow of death. It quickly gained on them with a speed that belied its size. Hikari angled upward, climbing higher into the sky. The beast continued to follow them, and Kai spotted a faint glow on its chest, a purple, pulsating light that reminded her of a heartbeat.

I have an idea, Kai said.

CHAPTER 7

They rose higher and higher, the clouds swirling in their wake. Kai watched the ground below shrink away. The air grew cold, biting at her face, and she shivered, her breath coming out in puffs.

Are you ready? Hikari asked.

Kai gripped the hilt of her sword, bracing herself.

Yes.

With a powerful thrust of her wings, the dragon soared into a patch of clouds. When she was certain the creature lost sight of them, Kai let go of Hikari. The wind whipped around her, screaming in her ears, and her cloak billowed out, fluttering like a shadow cast against the sky. She felt the fabric pulse with its strange magic, and she slipped into the shadow realm. Light bent and faded as she vanished, phasing into a world of shifting darkness.

She was still falling, but it was like falling through ink rather than air. The creature drew closer, and once it was within reach, Kai flickered back into the physical realm, reappearing just above the dragon's head, her sword raised high. Its eyes flared in shock at her sudden appearance, but it didn't have time to react.

Kai issued a fierce cry as she fell, driving her blade deep into the dragon's chest. It struck the pulsing purple light, and dark ichor spurted out, followed by a shockwave of energy. It erupted from the beast, burning her skin. She ignored the pain and pushed the sword deeper, locking eyes with the creature as it twisted its head to look down at her. For a brief moment, it stared back at her, something tortured and lost in its gaze.

With a guttural roar, the dragon flailed, its wings beating erratically as it plummeted toward the earth. Kai held her grip, willing every ounce of strength into her arms, and twisted the blade. The beast gave a gasp, its roar choked into silence as the darkness within it stilled. She jerked her blade free and kicked off from the beast just as Hikari swooped below, and she landed roughly on the dragon's back.

Well done, Hikari said. *But next time, perhaps something a little less dramatic.*

Kai couldn't help but smile at Hikari's teasing. They turned back toward the city, and Kai could see the Drakka were about to breach the walls. The Sworn and their dragons were trying to hold them off, but the horde of creatures was unending and their line of defense was riddled with gaps where soldiers had fallen.

Get me as close to the Drakka as you can.

Another plan? Hikari asked.

Yes, but less dramatic than the last one.

Hikari descended until she was gliding only a few feet above where the Drakka were gathered outside the walls. Kai tapped into the power of the Heart of Flame and directed it toward the ground, creating a fiery barrier. The heat seared the Drakka, forcing them to retreat. It was only a temporary reprieve, but it gave the Sworn time to clear the walls and regroup. Hikari landed behind the barrier as it began to fade.

There are so many, Kai said, staring at the legions of Drakka.

Hikari issued a wave of fire from her jaws, incinerating the enemies nearest to them.

It's not enough. We need to do more.

I'm open to suggestions, Hikari rumbled.

Kai could feel the elders of the past guiding her. She closed her eyes and took a deep breath, channeling the energy from the Heart. Simultaneously, she drew the shadows from the cloak, weaving the two together.

Release your flames again.

Hikari breathed her fire, bolstered by the Heart, and Kai released a surge of shadow energy. The two forces collided mid-air, intertwining in a mesmerizing dance of light and darkness.

The resulting blast was cataclysmic. A wave of searing heat and inky blackness swept across the battlefield, engulfing a vast swath of the Drakka forces. Their agonized screams were cut short as the devastating attack consumed them.

As the smoke cleared, Kai heard gasps and murmurs of awe from the Sworn on the walls. She caught sight of Jiro, his eyes wide with disbelief. Kai allowed herself a small smile, though her heart pounded with the effort of the attack.

The effect on the Drakka was immediate and profound. Their orderly ranks dissolved into chaos as the survivors scrambled to regroup. Kai watched with grim satisfaction as entire battalions turned tail and fled, their will to fight shattered.

"They're withdrawing," someone shouted.

The Drakka forces were in full retreat, their numbers dwindling with each passing moment. The Sworn, emboldened by this turn of events, pressed their advantage, driving the enemy further from the city walls. Victory was within reach, but Kai felt deep sorrow. So much life had been lost, both Drakka and man, and she knew the cost of this battle would be felt for generations to come.

The adrenaline that had fueled her throughout the battle was fading, leaving behind a bone-deep exhaustion that threatened to overwhelm her. Kai slumped forward against Hikari, her muscles screaming.

You need rest, Hikari said.

We're not done yet. If we let our guard down… she trailed off, too tired to finish the thought.

You've pushed yourself to your limit, the dragon replied, concern in her tone. *Rest, if only for a moment.*

"Kai?"

She turned to see Jiro and Ichiro. They had joined her on the battlefield, and their dragons regarded Hikari curiously.

"That was incredible," Ichiro said excitedly.

Jiro regarded his brother with raised eyebrows. "I would call it terrifying."

Kai smiled until she realized Jiro was serious.

"I thought we were about to lose the wall," Ichiro continued, "but you and your dragon turned the tide!"

Kai straightened, fighting against her fatigue. "Each of us played a part in this victory," she said softly.

"True, but you two made the difference. The way you wielded magic, how you and your dragon move as one... it was like watching a legend come to life."

Kai felt a warmth in her chest that had nothing to do with the Heart of Flame's power.

"You look pale," Jiro said. "You should probably get some rest."

With one last look at the battlefield, Kai nodded.

CHAPTER 8

Dawn found Kai standing motionless atop the wall, surveying the charred landscape. The smell of smoke still hung in the air, and she wrinkled her nose. Her armor, once gleaming, now bore the scars of battle. Her blade, however, remained sharp and as dark as when she'd first received it.

Master Satoshi joined her, his expression solemn. "You fought well last night."

Kai inclined her head. "Thank you, Master. I only wish I could have done more."

A commotion at the edge of the battlefield drew their attention. A lone rider approached at a breakneck speed, his horse's flanks lathered with sweat.

"A messenger," Master Satoshi murmured, his brows furrowing.

Kai glanced at the other Sworn who had gathered nearby, noting the tightening of jaws and the subtle shifting of stances. They, too, had sensed their hard-won triumph might be short-lived. The gates were opened for the rider, and Kai followed Master Satoshi down to the courtyard, her heart thundering. Had the emperor heard about her bond with Hikari?

The messenger's voice trembled as he delivered the news, each word landing like the blow of a hammer. "Zhencheng is under siege. A massive force of Drakka have descended without warning. The city's defenses are overwhelmed."

A collective gasp rippled through those standing within earshot. Kai's blood turned cold, her mind reeling at the implications. Zhencheng was the heart of the empire.

"How is this possible?" Master Satoshi asked, more to himself than the messenger. His face lit up with realization. "The attack here was a ruse."

"A ruse? Why would the Drakka send such a large force here for a ruse?" Kai asked.

"To divert our attention from their true target."

Akuhara's words came back to her. *The empire will crumble, and in its place will be something new, something better.*

"She seeks to kill the emperor," Kai said.

"It would seem so," Master Satoshi replied. "And we cannot allow that."

He immediately began issuing orders, and soon, Kai was standing alone. The power she shared with Hikari could save Zhencheng, and the emperor, but using it risked exposing her secret. Master Satoshi had been clear the emperor would kill her for breaking the law. Was saving the innocent worth the consequences?

Kai thought so. Hikari did, too, based on the approval she felt flowing through their bond. She made her way to the stable, where her fellow Sworn were already at work preparing to leave. The air held a nervous energy as dragons snorted and shifted, sensing the urgency.

"Can you hand me that salve?" Siran asked, pointing to one of the jars that lined a series of shelves behind her. Kai obliged, and

Siran applied the ointment to a gash on her dragon's flank.

"How is he faring?"

"He is strong, but this battle has taken its toll. I fear what we'll face in Zhencheng, especially without much rest."

Around them, the Sworn worked with efficiency. Armor was donned, supplies were packed, and weapons were gathered. Yet beneath the bustle, Kai sensed an undercurrent of fear—not just for themselves, but for the fate of the empire.

"Do you think we'll make it in time?" Ichiro asked, his usually jovial face etched with worry as he tightened his dragon's saddle.

Kai met his gaze, forcing a smile. "We have to try." She turned away from them, seeking a moment of solitude amidst the frantic preparations. She went to the stall where Hikari rested, her golden scales shimmering under the daylight that filtered in from the skylight overhead. The dragon lifted her head, her eyes meeting Kai's.

I am afraid, Kai admitted, sinking to the ground beside Hikari.

Afraid of what?

That I cannot defeat her.

The dragon rumbled softly in response, a wave of warmth and reassurance passing through the bond.

We will defeat her together, Hikari said. *We have overcome many challenges, and we will prevail over Akuhara as well. You are stronger than you know, and your heart is true.*

Kai drew strength from her words, and she nodded wordlessly. She reflected on the path that had brought her to this moment. Everything she had faced shaped her into who she was. Hikari was right, she was stronger than she realized. Master Satoshi's commanding voice cut through the air, drawing the Sworn to attention.

"Gather around," he said.

Kai joined the others, forming a tight circle around their leader.

"We fly into the heart of chaos against an enemy that outnumbers us." He paused, letting the gravity of his words sink in. "Our mission is to help the imperial army defend Zhencheng. If we cannot drive the Drakka back, then we must evacuate the emperor to safety."

Kai's mind conjured images of the capital under siege, nobles and commoners alike lying dead in the streets.

"Master," Jiro spoke up, bringing her back to the present. "How can we hope to succeed? Even if we get the emperor to safety, how long will that last before the Drakka come for him again? They will not give up the chase."

Master Satoshi's gaze hardened. "We are Sworn. Our strength lies not in our numbers, but in our unity, our determination. We will stand as one against this tide of darkness, and I have faith that we will rise above it."

A murmur of agreement rippled around the circle.

"We will need every Sworn and dragon at our disposal, which forces me to make an odd request. A few of us fell in battle last night, and although their dragons are grieving, we need soldiers who can command their power effectively. I trust each of you, and therefore I am relying on you to give me options. Who do you think is up to the task?"

Kai cleared her throat. "I know a few people."

CHAPTER 9

The Sworn formation cut through the sky like an arrow, speeding toward Zhencheng. The landscape stretched below them, a breathtaking display of countless hues blending together like a woven rug. Mountains loomed, their peaks disappearing into the clouds, and valleys cradled rivers that flowed like snakes across the land. Kai's heart swelled as she gazed upon the beauty of her homeland.

The wind whipped at her hair and tugged at her clothes, but it didn't bother her. She closed her eyes and stretched her arms out, relishing the freedom she felt. There were no worries in the sky, no fears or doubts plaguing her mind. There was only the rush of the wind and the beat of Hikari's wings.

They flew for most of the morning, and when the sun reached its zenith, Master Satoshi directed them to land. The group descended on the outskirts of a dense wooded area, and Kai dismounted, stretching her legs.

"Take some time to eat and rest," Master Satoshi said. "We'll continue shortly."

Kai thought it was odd he didn't order anyone to keep watch, but she decided the Drakka would be foolish to try to ambush them without a large force. She hadn't seen any sign of them from the sky, and she assumed that was because they were focused on the assault of the capital. Ryn approached her and bowed his head in respect.

"I am indebted to you again," he said.

"I didn't think you would agree," Kai replied. "Given your feelings for the empire, I mean."

Ryn looked past her to the trees and shrugged. "I would give anything to have my dragon back. This is the closest I'll ever get to that, so it was hard to decline."

"I understand. And the others?" She nodded toward the other Sundered, who kept themselves separated from the Sworn.

"They are of the same mind. We have been on our own for many years, and it is not easy being back among those whose loyalty lies with the empire. But we do not follow them. We follow you."

"I know you think it so, but I am not the Blooded One," Kai said softly.

"You may not carry the title, but you carry the spirit. You inspire hope where there is none, and your power is greater than any rider I have seen before. That is enough for me."

Kai was humbled by his words. Before she could respond, Ryn's eyes widened.

"Drakka!"

Kai whirled around and drew her sword, her eyes scanning the trees. "Where? I don't see anything."

"They are on the move. We need to stop them before they alert others."

Kai sprinted into the woods, weaving between the trees. She didn't need to go far before she spotted dark shapes moving through the underbrush. Following them, she burst through a bush, coming face to face with a Drakka scout. Without hesitation, she swung her blade. The Drakka blocked her strike and snarled, its eyes filled with malice.

Slipping into the shadows with the power of her cloak, Kai faded from view and reappeared behind the confused creature, thrusting her blade into its back. It gurgled and dropped to its knees. Placing her foot along its spine, Kai ripped her sword free and the Drakka fell face-first onto the ground. Siran and Jiro stood a few feet away, staring at her.

"Why are you just standing there? There are more of them. Hurry!"

Kai ran in the direction the other Drakka had fled in, and Siran and Jiro caught up to her. The three of them trailed after the Drakka, their steps thudding against the forest floor. Branches whipped at their faces and arms, but they pushed through the stinging pain, determined to catch the scouts before they alerted a larger force.

They chased the Drakka deeper into the woods, the undergrowth becoming denser as they went. The creatures moved swiftly, but they were hindered by the thick brush. As they rounded a bend, Kai skidded to a stop, holding out an arm to halt Siran and Jiro behind her. Through the trees, she could see a small clearing where a group of Drakka had gathered, their dark green scales blending with the colors of the forest. They appeared to be in the midst of a heated discussion, their snarls and hisses filling the air.

Kai crouched low, signaling for her companions to do the same. She knew they couldn't take on a group of Drakka this size on their own. They needed a plan.

Where are you? Kai asked Hikari.

I'm flying over the trees, but I can't see anything through the canopy. What's happening?

Kai sent an image of what she saw to the dragon, but Hikari only flooded the bond with her confusion. A twig snapped behind them, and the Drakka turned toward them. Kai jerked her head around to see Ichiro. He nodded at her before a whistling sound filled the air, and an arrow struck him in the chest.

He staggered back from the force and collapsed to the ground.

"Ichiro!" Jiro rushed to his brother's side.

The sound of battle filled the air, and Kai turned back to the clearing to see Ryn and the other Sundered fighting the Drakka. Siran charged into the clearing, sword flashing as she joined the fray.

Kai scrambled over to Ichiro. The arrow had struck perfectly within a gap in his armor. Blood was welling from the wound, and Kai pressed her hand against it to staunch the flow. Ichiro groaned in pain, and Jiro cradled his brother's head in his lap.

"Stay awake," he urged.

"We have to get him out of here. Master Satoshi will know what to do. Can you help me carry him?"

Jiro nodded and rose to his feet. Kai grabbed onto his legs and Jiro grabbed his arms, and together they carried him out of the woods. The camp was on high alert, and the Sworn were stationed on all sides, weapons drawn and ready.

Master Satoshi saw them as they exited the trees, and he called for a physician. Kai and Jiro set Ichiro down gently, and the physician took over, examining the wound. Without explaining anything, Kai sprinted back into the woods, heading for the clearing. When she returned, the Drakka were using their power over the earth, summoning tree roots from the ground to attack the Sundered.

Ryn and his men had exhausted their strength and were beginning to lose ground. Kai used her cloak to fade into the shadow realm, moving through the trees like a ghost and slaying one Drakka after another. The Sundered renewed their attack, and soon the entire group of creatures were dead.

"Is that all of them?" Kai asked after returning to the physical world.

Ryn tilted his head to the side as if he were listening to something, then nodded. "I don't sense any others. I think we killed them all."

Kai wiped her sword on one of the bodies and sheathed it. "Good. Did anyone suffer an injury?"

"No. We were lucky."

"Luck had nothing to do with it, I'm sure," she replied, smiling. "You are all skilled warriors."

Ryn bowed his head to her. They walked together through the woods, and when they returned to the camp, many of the Sworn gave Kai curious stares. She approached Master Satoshi.

"How is Ichiro?" she asked.

"He will survive, though he will not be able to fight. His dragon is going to take him back to Dangju."

Relief washed over Kai. "That is great news. Why is… everyone staring at me?"

"Word of your deeds in the woods is spreading."

"They're afraid of me now, aren't they?"

"Fear often stems from a lack of understanding," Master Satoshi said, placing a comforting hand on her shoulder. "Your secret is safe, do not worry about that. I will ensure they know you are no different than any other Sworn."

"Thank you, Master," she whispered.

"Eat something and prepare yourself. We need to press on."

The journey resumed, and they flew until night, making camp on a plateau among the mountains. Kai's exhaustion led to the first full night of rest she had experienced in days. Just before dawn broke, Master Satoshi roused them all, offering them steamed rice for breakfast before ordering them back on the move.

They flew for several hours, and as Zhencheng came into view on the horizon, a sudden gust of wind buffeted them, causing the dragons to sway precariously. Kai's grip on Hikari tightened as she squinted ahead.

Something isn't right, she told her dragon. *This isn't natural.*

No sooner had the words left her mind than a wall of swirling clouds materialized before them, crackling with purple lightning. The storm appeared out of nowhere, its intensity reminding Kai of the storm that had battered Ikje before the Ceremony of Oaths.

Drakka magic, Hikari said. *I can sense it.*

Kai knew they couldn't turn back, not when they were so close. Drawing upon their bond, she reached out with her senses, probing the magical storm.

I think I can guide us through it, she said. *Take us up to Master Satoshi.*

The dragon sped up, taking them to the lead position.

"Let me take the lead!" she shouted, trying to be heard above the wind. "Tell them to follow me!"

Master Satoshi nodded, waving them onward. Hikari took point, and the Sworn fell into position behind them. Kai closed her eyes, focusing on the ebb and flow of the magical energies surrounding them. *Can you sense it?* she asked the dragon.

Yes. The path is treacherous, but not impassable.

With a deep breath, Kai opened her eyes and urged Hikari forward, diving into the heart of the storm. Lightning crackled around them, the wind threatening to tear them from the sky. But Kai remained focused, guiding the group through the maelstrom with a combination of instinct and her magical abilities.

Left! she said, and Hikari banked sharply, narrowly avoiding a tendril of purple lightning. *Now up!*

For what felt like an eternity, they navigated the magical tempest until, finally, with a last burst of speed, they emerged on the other side, the storm dissipating behind them. Cheers erupted from the Sworn as they realized they'd made it through the storm. Master Satoshi retook the lead. He glanced at her, his lips curled into a small, satisfied smile. There was something deeply personal about it, as though the pride bloomed not for anyone else's eyes but her own.

Kai nodded at him in return, her chest tight with a mix of exhilaration and unease. She knew her powers were growing, but at what cost?

The landscape below grew desolate. Scorched earth and abandoned villages told the tale of the Drakka's advance. Kai's mood grew somber. The once-verdant lands surrounding the capital were now a wasteland, and in the distance, she could see the faint glow of fires.

How many innocents have suffered already? she wondered.

Hikari's reassuring presence filled her mind. *We will avenge them.*

In the distance, the imposing walls of Zhencheng finally came into view, but instead of being a beacon of hope, they now stood as a last bastion against the encroaching darkness. The Drakka horde's presence was unmistakable, their war machines and dark magic a plague on the land. Kai swallowed hard, steeling herself for the battle to come.

If we fall... she trailed off.

If we fall, we will do so in a blaze of glory, Hikari said.

CHAPTER 10

The great city of Zhencheng stood before Akuhara like a stubborn ember refusing to be snuffed out. Its high walls bristled with imperial soldiers, and Sworn flew overhead. Even from the ridge where she stood, she could see the banners of the emperor flapping defiantly in the wind, their golden threads shimmering in the light.

Her forces gathered below, a seething mass of Drakka that filled the air with their snarls and growls. She had summoned every last one of them, from the smallest hatchlings to the mightiest warriors. This was to be her final strike, the crushing blow that would end the empire once and for all. And yet, her fists clenched with rage.

Dangju. The name burned in her mind like a brand. When the news of the Drakka's defeat there had reached her, she had screamed out in anger and frustration. A city that should have been reduced to ash now still stood, thanks to the intervention of her sister.

Kai.

Akuhara turned sharply, seething with fury as she strode into her tent. The space was illuminated with a brazier that burned brightly, the glow casting shadows across the maps and battle plans sprawled on the table. Her dragon followed, sticking his head through the tent flaps, its molten eyes gleaming with curiosity and concern.

You let your rage consume you, it said, its voice a low rumble.

Be silent, Akuhara snapped, slamming her hands onto the table. Her breath came in short, furious bursts as she stared at the map of Zhencheng. Her claws of dark magic traced the city's defenses, searching for weaknesses, for any crack she could exploit.

She's here, Akuhara said finally, her voice trembling with a mix of anger and something she didn't want to admit. Fear. *Kai has brought more Sworn to defend the city. She's grown stronger. Too strong.*

The dragon stretched closer, its massive head close enough that she could feel his breath. *You have faced her before. You can face her again. And this time, you will defeat her.*

Akuhara shook her head, her hands balling into fists. *She's different now. Every time, she becomes more than what I expect. More than what I can overcome. She has an elder dragon, and now she has the Heart of Flame and that cloak. How am I supposed to stop that?*

The dragon's molten eyes narrowed. *You have an entire horde at your command. You have me. She is but one.*

"She is not just one!" Akuhara shouted aloud, slamming her fist against the table hard enough to crack the wood. She drew in a ragged breath, her shoulders trembling. *She is cut from the same cloth I am. And she will not stop until she has won.*

Silence hung in the air, thick and suffocating. Akuhara turned away, her gaze drifting to the back of the tent. Outside, the roars of the Drakka echoed through the encampment, their bloodlust palpable. She knew she could unleash them, let them overwhelm the city in a tide of fire and destruction. But it wouldn't just be the empire that fell. It would be everything. Possibly even her.

"I have to end this," Akuhara whispered, her voice barely audible. "No more retreats. No more waiting. Zhencheng must burn."

Her dragon rumbled in agreement, but there was a note of caution in its tone. *Then you must steel yourself. She will not show mercy. And neither can you.*

Akuhara straightened, her expression hardening into a mask of resolve. She left the tent, her mind churning with doubt and fear, but she buried it deep beneath the weight of her anger. If she was to face Kai again, it would be on her terms. And this time, she would not falter.

She magically projected her voice, her tone cold and unyielding.

"Attack!"

CHAPTER 11

The smell of smoke stung Kai's nostrils as they circled above the imperial city. War drums reverberated through the air, mingling with the guttural roars of the Drakka—a relentless tide that stretched as far as the horizon. Their hulking forms churned the earth into a foul mire, destroying everything underfoot.

Imperial soldiers stood atop the walls, their faces pale but their weapons steady. Archers loosed volleys of arrows, though many found no purchase on the Drakka's thick, armored hides. Siege engines hurled flaming pitch and vats of boiling oil were poured onto the attackers, but the sheer mass of the enemy was undiminished. For every Drakka that fell, a dozen more surged forward, climbing over the corpses of their own kind in their insatiable hunger to breach the city.

And somewhere out there, Kai knew, was her sister. She viewed it all with a grim expression, hope slowly giving way to despair.

How can we hope to turn back such a tide? she asked.

We have no other choice but to succeed, Hikari replied.

Master Satoshi returned from speaking with the emperor, his dragon flying to the center of their formation. He shouted to be heard above the noise, his voice cutting through the chaos.

"The emperor has given us one final order: we are to break through the Drakka lines and cut the head from the snake." As he spoke, he looked at Kai. "We must draw her out and defeat her by any means necessary."

Kai knew the true meaning behind his words: she was tasked with stopping Akuhara. She offered a silent nod of acceptance. They had battled once before, and while Kai had won, her sister's power was not to be underestimated.

Any ideas on how to find her? Hikari asked.

Kai scanned the Drakka's ranks, but there was no sign of Akuhara. *We need to do something to gain her attention.*

"I'll need the Sundered," Kai told Master Satoshi.

"Take whoever you need. The rest of us will do what we can to keep the Drakka away from the walls."

Kai motioned to Ryn, and Hikari descended from the sky, releasing a torrent of flame that carved a swath through the Drakka, incinerating dozens in a single breath. Behind her, the Sundered followed. Ryn led his men on a midnight-black dragon, striking like a shadowy harbinger of death. The Sundered flew in a tight formation, their blades flashing and magic crackling as they dove into the fray.

Kai clung to Hikari's saddle, her hair whipping in the wind as they dove toward a group of Drakka. With a wordless cry, she unleashed the Heart of Flame, the artifact flaring in her grasp. A fiery shockwave erupted, scattering the creatures like leaves in a storm. But the creatures were relentless, and Hikari wheeled upward as Drakka swarmed toward them, their talons raking the air.

Kai looked for her sister, but she was nowhere to be found. Her eyes narrowed as she saw a massive Drakka—a creature twice the size of its kin—charging toward the city's outer gate. Its flesh gleamed like obsidian, and a crown of twisted horns adorned its head.

I don't know what that is, but it can't be good, Kai said.

Should we try to stop it? Hikari asked.

Kai hesitated. *No. We need to find Akuhara.*

Hikari surged higher into the smoke-filled sky, her wings beating with powerful strokes as the sounds of battle below grew dimmer. Kai scanned the battlefield, but Akuhara was still nowhere to be seen.

We need a distraction big enough to draw Akuhara out. Something she can't ignore.

Before she could decide what that might be, she noticed the Drakka were swarming to one side of the walls. It wasn't chaos, it was coordinated, almost as if—

Her heart sank as she spotted it: a breach in the wall. Drakka were pouring through like water from a broken dam. "No," she whispered, her mind racing. They couldn't lose the city. Kai made a split-second decision.

Take me down there, she told Hikari, gripping the dragon tightly as they did a spiraling dive down toward the wall. They landed amidst the Drakka horde, and Hikari let out a deafening roar. The Drakka faltered for a moment, and Kai wasted no time in channeling the Heart of Flame, unleashing a wave of fire that consumed the nearest enemies in an inferno.

Hikari breathed her own flames, and with a primal growl, Kai thrust her hands forward, guiding the fire toward her dragon's flames. The two streams merged, growing, twisting, until a massive wall of searing heat erupted before them.

The Drakka's advance halted abruptly, their war cries turning to screams of confusion and pain. The barrier of fire stretched across the breach, an impenetrable curtain of flickering orange and gold. Kai's arms trembled with the effort of maintaining the spell. She was buying them time to seal the breach, but she knew it wouldn't be enough.

Her gaze swept across the walls, taking in the battered defenses, the exhausted soldiers, and the relentless enemy that still pressed against her fiery barrier. A sudden, bone-chilling roar echoed through the chaos.

Kai's heart skipped a beat as she turned to see the massive obsidian Drakka charging towards them, its horns gleaming in the firelight. The other Drakka in the vicinity seemed to part like a dark sea, making way for the formidable creature. Its eyes locked onto Kai, and a shiver ran down her spine. This Drakka was no ordinary beast; it exuded an aura of power and malevolence that made even Hikari falter for a moment.

Just as she felt her strength slipping, Ryn and the other Sundered joined the fray, attacking the enormous Drakka. Their dragons unleashed torrents of flame, lightning, and ice, their ferocity unmatched.

But it wasn't enough. The Drakka were too many, their ranks too deep. Even the Sundered's heroics couldn't tilt the balance for long. They needed a miracle.

CHAPTER 12

"The breach is sealed!" Master Satoshi shouted.

It was a small victory, but it bolstered Kai's spirit nonetheless. She turned her attention back to the enormous Drakka. At the risk of breaking her concentration, she slipped off the dragon's back and stood beside her.

Help me take him down, Kai said to Hikari.

I'm ready when you are.

"Ryn!" Kai shouted. "Pull back!"

He did as she asked, and the other Sundered followed his command to do the same. With them out of the way, Kai turned the flames from the wall toward the Drakka, forcing the wall to enclose around the creature. The Drakka clawed at the barrier, its massive form silhouetted against the flames. Its roars of defiance turned to pained cries as the flames seared its flesh, but still, it pushed forward with unnatural strength. Kai gritted her teeth and focused all her energy on maintaining the spell, her body trembling with exertion.

With a thunderous roar, Hikari lunged forward through the wall of fire, crashing into the Drakka. Their clash sent shockwaves through the ground beneath Kai as they grappled for dominance. Kai released the magic and drew her sword, hesitating as her vision swam. It quickly cleared and she rushed ahead, swinging her blade in an arc that separated the Drakka's head from its shoulders. A cheer rose from the defenders on the walls.

But the fight wasn't over yet. More Drakka surged forward, their hatred fueled by the fall of their comrade. A host of Sworn and their dragons landed on either side of Kai, joining the battle. Kai climbed onto Hikari's back, and the Sworn shifted into an arrowhead formation. Kai felt Hikari's muscles tense beneath her, ready to lead the charge.

"Together!" Kai shouted.

"Together!" the others echoed in unison.

The air filled with the clash of battle as dragons and Drakka collided. Kai guided Hikari with subtle shifts of her weight, their minds working as one. They pressed into the Drakka'a ranks, striking quick, deadly blows, leaving destruction in their wake.

The tide of battle began to shift, slowly but inexorably. Kai watched with growing elation as the Drakka's lines started to fracture under the Sworn's relentless assault. Streams of fire, ice, and lightning arced through the sky as the Sworn unleashed their elemental powers in perfect harmony.

Kai felt a surge of pride and hope. Feeling bold, she experimented with the cloak's capabilities by extending its power to cover Hikari as well. She succeeded, but it took a toll on her. She used it in bursts, guiding Hikari through the shadow realm to appear where they were needed most, reappearing to offer support and direction.

"They're faltering!" Kai called out, her heart racing. "Keep pressing!"

As if in response to her words, the Drakka's formations began to crumble. Their fearsome roars turned to shrieks of frustration and pain as they found themselves outmaneuvered at every turn. A horn blasted through the air, and the Drakka began to retreat.

Akuhara is close, Kai said. *Take me up.*

Hikari took to the air, and Kai scanned the ground. There was still no sign of her sister. She watched the waves of Drakka pull back from the city, but she knew it was only a brief respite. As long as Akuhara was out there, the Drakka would not relent. They returned to the ground, and Master Satoshi was waiting among the Sworn.

"You have proven yourself a leader," he said to Kai. "The Sworn rallied to you on their own."

"I was only doing what any of us would do," Kai replied.

"We must rally our forces and prepare for the next wave. What we've seen is only the beginning."

Master Satoshi was right. The next wave of Drakka would arrive, and once again, the city's defenses would be tested to their limits. They needed rest, but there was no time to waste. Master Satoshi began issuing orders, organizing their forces and preparing for the impending onslaught.

It wasn't long before a scout arrived with the news that the Drakka had regrouped.

"How many?" Master Satoshi asked.

"More than before. Far more." The scout's voice quavered. "And the sky... it's not natural."

Dark storm clouds swirled on the horizon, tinged with an eerie green glow. A low rumble shook the ground, as if the earth itself trembled in fear. In the distance, a vast sea of shadows appeared on the horizon, stretching as far as the eye could see. The Drakka had returned.

As Kai watched, a figure rose above the ranks, terrible and familiar. Akuhara. Beside her loomed a monstrous shape—her dragon, wreathed in green light and flame. The air grew heavy, charged with an oppressive energy that made it hard to breathe. Kai felt a presence at her side and turned to see Siran, her face grave.

"By the ancestors," she breathed. "There are so many..."

The storm clouds roiled overhead, and in the distance, Akuhara's dragon let out a bone-chilling roar. Kai closed her eyes, reaching deep within herself for the strength she would need in the coming battle. The elements answered her call, fire and earth surging through her veins.

I am with you, Hikari said. *We will defeat her together.*

Master Satoshi's voice cut through the tension, drawing Kai from her thoughts. He stood atop a nearby battlement, his hair whipping in the wind as he addressed the gathered defenders.

"Sons and daughters of Zhencheng!" he bellowed. "The enemy stands at our gates, but they shall find no easy victory here! We are the guardians of this land, and our spirits burn brighter than their dark clouds! Remember those who came before us, who gave their lives so that we might stand here today! We are Sworn, and we will not falter!"

A chorus of cheers erupted from the defenders. Kai raised her fist in solidarity, her heart pounding with a mix of fear and determination. She ran a hand along Hikari's scales. The dragon rumbled in response, a plume of smoke curling from her nostrils.

A deafening crash shook the foundations of the city. In the distance, massive boulders arced through the air, smashing against Zhencheng's outer walls.

"They've brought siege engines!" someone shouted.

Kai's mind raced. "Hikari, we need to—"

Before she could finish her sentence, another volley slammed into the defenses. The air filled with the screams of panicked civilians and the shouts of soldiers rushing to their posts.

"Multiple breaches!" came a frantic cry from beyond the wall. "They're attacking from all sides!"

CHAPTER 13

The world blurred as Hikari took flight, her powerful wings carrying them above the chaos. From their vantage point, Kai's heart sank at the sight below. The outer walls had crumbled in several places, and streams of Drakka forces poured through the gaps like a toxic flood.

We can't let them reach the palace, Kai said.

Hikari growled in agreement, diving towards the nearest breach. Kai called forth gouts of flame to rain down upon the invaders. Screams of pain and rage echoed up from below. As they banked for another pass, Kai caught sight of terrified civilians fleeing through the streets.

We need to buy them time, she said, more to herself than to Hikari. *Head for the main gate!*

They soared over the city, Kai's stomach twisting at the destruction below. Fires raged unchecked, smoke billowing into the sky. The sound of clashing steel and agonized cries filled the air. Landing near the gate, Kai leapt from Hikari's back.

"Where is Master Satoshi?" she asked a nearby guard.

"He was summoned by the emperor."

Hold this position, she told Hikari.

Kai ran through the streets. The Drakka's assault was relentless, far beyond what she had imagined. She reached the palace and strode in without challenge as the guards were absent. As she burst into the imperial chambers, the scene before her made her blood run cold.

The emperor, his face ashen, was surrounded by cowering advisors. "We have no choice," he was saying, his aged voice trembling. "We must surrender before all is lost."

"Your Majesty!" Kai shouted, striding forward. All eyes turned to her, including Master Satoshi's who stood next to the emperor's throne. "You can't surrender."

The emperor's eyes narrowed. "Zhencheng is falling. To continue this fight is to doom our people to slaughter."

Kai shook her head vehemently. "I can stop this. I can face Akuhara directly."

Master Satoshi leaned in close and whispered into the emperor's ear. Kai couldn't help but wonder if he was betraying her. The emperor studied her for a long moment, conflict clear on his face. Finally, he nodded.

"I won't fail," she promised. "Keep the emperor safe," she added, looking at Master Satoshi. He nodded, and Kai left the palace, sprinting back toward the main gate of the city.

It's time to end this, she told Hikari as she slid to a halt beside the dragon. *I'll deal with Akuhara. You keep her beast busy.*

Hikari took flight with a loud roar, disappearing over the wall. Kai slipped through the gate, which had been pushed ajar by a large boulder. She scanned the battlefield and found Akuhara leading a group of Drakka, power crackling around her like a sinister aura. Kai tightened her grip on her hilt and rushed out to meet her.

"I should have known I'd find you here," her sister said. "You've become quite a thorn in my side."

"Allow me to ease your suffering."

Without warning, Akuhara struck. Dark tendrils of magic, intertwined with searing flames, lashed out towards Kai. She barely had time to react. She dove to the side, channeling her connection to the earth. The ground trembled, responding to her will. A wall of stone burst from the ground, shielding her from the worst of Akuhara's onslaught.

"You can't beat me," Akuhara taunted, unleashing another barrage of dark fire that melted the stone. "You're too weak, too afraid to seize true power!"

Gritting her teeth, Kai drew upon the Heart of Flame's magic, pushing her sister's flames aside. "You're wrong," she replied, her voice steady despite the strain. "Strength isn't about domination. It's about doing what's right, even when it costs you everything."

Akuhara's eyes flashed with malice as she summoned a whirlwind of shadows, her fingers twisting in arcane gestures. "Such noble sentiments won't save you or this empire. I told you before, I'm going to burn this world and create something new."

The dark tempest surged towards Kai, crackling with energy. Kai's instincts took over. She thrust her hands forward, calling upon the Heart of Flame. A brilliant wall of fire erupted before her, intertwining with wisps of shadow she conjured from the shadow realm.

"I won't let you destroy anything else!" Kai shouted.

Their powers clashed in a dazzling spectacle. Streams of fire and shadow danced around them, the air sizzling with energy. Kai drew upon the earth, causing the ground to shift and buckle beneath Akuhara's feet. Her sister stumbled but quickly regained her footing, retaliating with a torrent of water from the sky that threatened to drown Kai where she stood. Kai countered the magic by super-heating the air, turning the deluge to steam.

"Clever," Akuhara grudgingly admitted, her eyes narrowing. "But you are a novice compared to me."

Kai's breath came in short gasps. She could feel the strain of maintaining such intense elemental manipulation. But she couldn't falter now. With a swift motion, Kai summoned a gust of wind, using it to propel herself into the air. From this vantage point, she rained down a barrage of fireballs, each one aimed at pushing Akuhara back.

She couldn't keep this up much longer.

Kai felt the familiar warmth of Hikari's presence brush against her mind. In that moment of connection, a surge of strength flooded through her. She closed her eyes briefly, drawing a deep breath.

Show her your true power.

The words came from their bond, but it wasn't Hikari voice she heard. It was Kokoro's. With a fluid motion, Kai unfurled the dragon skin cloak, its scales shimmering with an otherworldly light. As she wrapped it around herself, she slipped into the shadow realm. The battlefield around her became muted, ghostly. She could see Akuhara, but her sister's movements were sluggish, as if she were moving through water.

Kai darted through the shadows, emerging behind Akuhara. She kicked the back of her leg, dropping her sister to her knees. Akuhara rose and whirled around, but Kai was already gone, melting back into the shadows. She reappeared at Akuhara's left, summoning a whirlwind of fire that caught her twin off guard.

"Stand still and fight me!" Akuhara roared.

Kai felt a pang of sadness. "I am fighting you," she said. "But on my terms, not yours!"

As she danced between realms, Kai could feel the tide of battle shifting. Akuhara's attacks, once so overwhelming, now seemed clumsy and predictable. With each pass, Kai used the elements—fire to blind, earth to trap, and air to buffet.

Akuhara's fury grew with each failed assault. "You think your parlor tricks can save you?" she screamed, unleashing a massive wave of dark energy.

But Kai was ready. She emerged from the shadows directly in front of her sister, her hands weaving an intricate pattern, guided by the elder dragons of the past. The elements responded to her call, forming a shimmering barrier that absorbed Akuhara's attack.

With a gesture, she turned Akuhara's own dark energy against her, sending it crashing back in a dazzling display. For the first time, Kai saw fear flicker in her sister's eyes. With a bone-chilling scream, Akuhara thrust her hands skyward. The air crackled as darkness swirled around her, coalescing into a maelstrom of pure destructive force.

Kai closed her eyes, placing a hand over the Heart of Flame. Its warmth pulsed in sync with her heartbeat, and she felt Hikari's strength flowing through her. With a deep breath, Kai channeled the Heart of Flame's power. Fire erupted from her hands, meeting Akuhara's assault head-on. The clash of energies lit up the battlefield, casting eerie shadows across the city's walls.

Kai gritted her teeth, her arms trembling with the effort. Slowly, inch by inch, Kai's fire began to push back against Akuhara's darkness. The air shimmered with heat, the ground beneath their feet splintering from the immense pressure.

The Heart of Flame blazed brighter than ever, its power coursing through Kai's veins. With tears streaming down her face, she gathered her strength for one final push, but as the flames engulfed Akuhara, her resolve wavered.

CHAPTER 14

Despite everything, a flicker of hope burned within Kai. She extended her hand, her voice soft yet urgent.

"Abandon this path," she pleaded. "It doesn't have to end this way."

Akuhara's lips curled into a sneer, her voice dripping with venom. "You naive child. The darkness is all I have."

With a snarl, Akuhara lunged forward, dark energy crackling around her fingertips. Kai's instincts kicked in, her elemental powers surging forth. She thrust her hands outward, invisible forces pinning Akuhara to the ground.

Kai's heart pounded like a drum, refusing to slow. Was this truly the only way? But as she gazed into Akuhara's hate-filled eyes, she knew there was no other choice.

With a heavy heart, Kai unsheathed her black-bladed sword. The weight of it felt different now, as if it carried the burden of what she must do. She raised the blade high, its obsidian surface reflecting the chaos around them.

Akuhara struggled against her invisible tethers, but it was no use.

"I'm sorry," Kai whispered. Their eyes met, and Kai drove the sword deep into Akuhara's heart.

A terrible scream tore from Akuhara's throat, darkness exploding outward. Kai stumbled back, her eyes wide as she watched the light fade from her sister's gaze. Her dragon roared in pain and broke away from Hikari, flying awkwardly before crashing to the ground in a shower of dust. Hikari streaked through the sky, landing atop the fallen dragon and ending his thrashing.

As Akuhara's body went limp, a ripple of uncertainty passed through the Drakka forces. Kai could sense their faltering resolve, but knew the danger was far from over. Their leader had fallen, but they still threatened to overwhelm the city.

Kai closed her eyes, reaching deep within herself. She felt the warm pulse of her bond with Hikari, the fiery energy of the Heart of Flame, and the ancient power of the dragon-skin cloak on her shoulders. The elements swirled around her, responding to her call.

"No more," Kai declared, her voice carrying across the battlefield. She began to weave the disparate energies together, guided by ancient knowledge that funneled through the bond.

As the power built within her, Kai's thoughts turned to the weight of her duty. How many lives hung in the balance? How much would be sacrificed to secure peace? The questions burned in her mind as she channeled every ounce of her strength into her impending strike.

Her eyes snapped open, blazing with an otherworldly light. The combined power of the elements and shadows surged through her, burning brighter and fiercer than anything she'd felt before. It was as if every fiber of her being had become a conduit for pure, unbridled energy.

Hikari howled with anguish, the dragon's pain and determination echoing Kai's own. Their bond, already strong, deepened to an almost unbearable level. Kai could feel Hikari's heartbeat as if it were her own, their minds melding until she wasn't sure where she ended and the dragon began.

I don't know if I can contain this, Kai cried out to Hikari.

Your strength is mine, and mine is yours. Take what you need.

As the power continued to build, Kai felt a searing pain across her back. The cloak began to tear under the strain of the elemental forces coursing through it. With each rip, Kai felt her connection to the elements fracture, threatening to slip away entirely.

Despite the agony ripping through her body and the danger of losing control, Kai pressed on. She raised her hands, channeling every ounce of power she could muster. The very fabric of reality seemed to warp around her.

With a final, earth-shattering cry, Kai released the pent-up energy. A fiery explosion of magic erupted from her hands, engulfing the Drakka forces in a blinding inferno. The power was overwhelming, beautiful, and terrifying all at once.

As the magic poured out of her, Kai felt her consciousness begin to slip. Her thoughts turned to Hikari, of the unbreakable bond they shared, and she found comfort.

The deafening roar of the explosion faded, giving way to an eerie silence. As the smoke began to dissipate, Kai blinked, her vision blurry and unfocused. The bitter smell of ash and smoke filled her nostrils, making her cough weakly.

Hikari?

A low rumble answered her, and Kai felt the comforting presence of her dragon nearby. As her vision cleared, she saw the devastation that surrounded them. The army of Drakka lay in ruins, war machines crumbled and bodies torn asunder. She turned to Zhencheng and signs of life began to emerge.

Survivors, their faces streaked with soot and disbelief, cautiously peeked out from hiding places. A child's cry pierced the air, followed by the relieved sob of a mother. Slowly, people began to gather, their eyes fixed on Kai and Hikari with a mixture of awe and gratitude.

An elderly man approached, his robes tattered and covered in blood. "You... you saved us," he said, his voice trembling. "The Drakka... they're gone."

Kai tried to respond, but her strength was fading rapidly. The world began to spin, and she felt herself falling. *Hikari*, she reached out with her mind. *I can't...*

As consciousness slipped away, Kai felt the warm embrace of Hikari's wing enveloping her. The dragon's presence in her mind was a soothing balm, even as pain wracked both their bodies.

Rest, Hikar's voice echoed in her thoughts. *You have done more than enough. Zhencheng is safe.*

Kai's last coherent thought was of the immense toll their victory had taken. As darkness claimed her, she wondered if the price of peace would ever truly be paid in full.

CHAPTER 15

As consciousness slowly returned, Kai's fingers instinctively sought the familiar texture of her cloak. Instead, they met tattered remnants, the once-powerful garment now reduced to frayed edges and gaping holes. She forced her eyes open, wincing at the effort.

"The cloak," she whispered, her voice hoarse. "It's..."

Hikari's rumbling voice filled her mind. *A casualty of our victory.*

Kai struggled to sit up, her body protesting every movement. She held the ruined cloak before her, its magical essence was gone, dissipated like mist in the morning sun. As she grappled with the loss, she felt her connection to the elements dim, like a candle guttering in the wind.

I can feel it, Kai said, a lump forming in her throat. *The elements... they're slipping away.*

Kai reached out with her senses. The earth beneath her felt muted, the air less responsive to her call. It was as if a part of herself had been torn away, leaving a hollow ache in its wake.

Was it worth it? she asked.

The dragon's eyes met hers, filled with a mixture of sorrow and pride. *Look around you. The city stands. Its people live. What is the price of a cloak compared to that?*

Kai nodded slowly, her fingers tracing the remnants of the magical garment. *You're right, of course. It's just...*

Her words were cut short by the sound of trumpets. The makeshift curtain of her recovery tent was drawn back, revealing an imperial messenger in resplendent, if slightly singed, robes.

"Kai Lin," the messenger announced, bowing deeply. "His Imperial Majesty requests your presence for a ceremony of honor. You and your dragon are to be celebrated as the saviors of Zhencheng."

Kai exchanged a glance with Hikari. *I'm not sure I'm in any condition for a ceremony,* she admitted.

The dragon's amusement rippled through their bond.

How long have I been unconscious?

A few days, Hikari replied. *They've been checking on you every hour to see if you've woken. They're desperate to pay honor to you.*

Kai wasn't sure how she felt about that, but she gingerly rose from her bed anyway. She made herself as presentable as possible and glanced around the tent curiously.

I wouldn't let them move you out of my sight, Hikari said, reading her thoughts. *They set this up where you collapsed.*

Kai laughed and immediately regretted it as pain flashed through her body. She winced, waiting for it to pass before stepping out of the tent. She followed the messenger, and Hikari stayed close behind her.

They entered what remained of the imperial palace, and Kai was surprised to see a large crowd filtering in for the ceremony.

The throne room's ceiling was open to the sky, its roof nothing more than a memory. Her parents were there, and tears filled her eyes. With all of the chaos, she hadn't thought to ask Master Satoshi about them.

The emperor rose from his throne and stepped forward. "Kai Lin," he intoned, his voice carrying to every corner of the room. "You have done what many thought impossible. You have saved not just this city, but the very heart of our empire."

Kai bowed her head, feeling the weight of every gaze upon her. "Your Majesty, I—"

"No," the emperor interrupted, a smile gracing his features. "Today, it is we who bow to you." To Kai's astonishment, the emperor lowered himself to his knees, then pressed his head down to the ground at her feet in a gesture of deep respect.

As he straightened, the emperor's eyes gleamed with pride. "Kai Lin, your bravery and leadership have proven invaluable. I would have you stand among my council, to help guide our empire into this new era of peace."

A murmur of approval rippled through the crowd. Kai felt her heart racing, torn between duty and the nagging feeling that her path lay elsewhere. She glanced at Hikari, seeking guidance in her eyes.

"Your Majesty," Kai began, her voice steady despite her inner turmoil. "I am deeply honored by your offer..." She took a deep breath, feeling the weight of her decision. "...but I must respectfully decline." A collective gasp rippled through the crowd, and even the emperor's eyebrows raised in surprise.

"My path," Kai continued, her voice growing stronger, "lies not in the halls of power, but among the people I've sworn to protect. The war may be over, but the scars it left run deep. I wish to help rebuild what has been lost, to ensure that the lessons of this conflict are not forgotten. The threat of the Drakka isn't gone, not fully. There are nests out there that must be found and destroyed. These things are my path. With all due respect, I do not wish to be a figurehead on your council."

She met the emperor's gaze. "Your Majesty, you have the power to lead our people into a new era of peace and unity without me."

The emperor nodded slowly, a look of understanding dawning on his face. "Your wisdom continues to impress me, Kai Lin. Very well, I shall honor your decision."

Food was brought out from the royal kitchen, and Kai sat with her parents as they ate together. They spoke little, choosing instead to enjoy their time together. As the ceremony concluded, Kai felt a mixture of relief and anticipation. She turned to Hikari, who had been a silent presence throughout.

Are you ready for another journey?

Hikari's rumble was answer enough. She bade her family goodbye, and set out from Zhencheng with Ryn and the Sundered, leaving behind the cheers and accolades for the open sky.

As they traveled, the landscape gradually transformed. The scorched earth gave way to tender shoots of grass, and the smell of smoke was replaced by the sweet scent of wildflowers. Kai marveled at nature's resilience, feeling a spark of hope with each sign of renewal.

In a small village, they paused to rest. Kai watched as villagers worked together to rebuild homes, their faces etched with determination rather than despair. A young girl approached, offering Kai and her companions a handful of freshly picked berries.

"For the dragon rider who saved us," the child said, her eyes wide with admiration.

Kai accepted the gift with a smile, her throat tight with emotion. "Thank you," she murmured, realizing that this—this moment of simple kindness—was why she had accepted this path.

As they continued their journey, Kai's thoughts drifted to the challenges that lay ahead. Once the nests were destroyed, she wanted to repair Tatenagawa. The temple's restoration would be no small task, but she knew it was necessary. It would stand as a beacon of hope, a reminder of what could be achieved when people stood united against darkness.

CHAPTER 16

As the days turned to weeks, Ryn sensed less of the Drakka eggs. They had destroyed over a dozen nests, and now they stood outside the entrance of the last one. The cavern loomed ahead of them, its jagged mouth yawning open as though the earth itself had split apart to spill its dark secrets. Kai stood at the entrance, her hand resting on the hilt of her sword. The air was thick with a cloying, sulfuric smell that made her stomach churn. Hikari shifted beside her, her golden scales glinting faintly in the light filtering through the stormy sky.

Behind them, the Sundered waited in silence. Ryn stepped forward, his face grim. "This is the largest nest we've found so far," he said, his voice low. "As soon as we can destroy this one, the Drakka threat will end for good."

Kai nodded, her gaze fixed on the darkness ahead. "We are almost done," she said. Her voice was steady, but a flicker of unease danced at the edge of her thoughts. Each nest they had destroyed had exacted its toll—on their strength, and on their spirits. For some reason she could not explain, destroying the eggs became a weight upon her, upon them all, that they could not ignore. She suspected it was a curse of some kind, perhaps an enchantment left behind by Akuhara.

Hikari's rumbling voice broke through her thoughts. *The eggs will not resist, but the act itself will strain you. You must be ready.*

I am, Kai said, her grip tightening on her sword. "We've come too far to falter now." Those last words were aimed at Ryn as she glanced over her shoulder.

Ryn nodded, signaling the others. The Sundered fell into formation, their weapons drawn. They were fewer now than when she had first met them. Each loss weighed on Kai's heart, but she pushed the grief aside.

There would be time to mourn when the last remnants of the Drakka were gone.

The group moved into the cavern, the darkness swallowing them whole. The walls were slick with moisture, and the air grew warmer with each step. The faint, rhythmic pulsing of the eggs echoed through the chamber, a sound that sent a shiver down Kai's spine.

The nest was vast, its floor littered with clusters of eggs. Their translucent shells pulsed faintly with an ominous light.

"Spread out," Kai ordered.

The Sundered moved into position. Hikari unleashed a controlled stream of fire, the flames washing over the eggs. The outer shells hissed and cracked under the heat, the light within them flickering like dying embers.

Kai stepped forward, her sword raised, and brought it down in a clean strike. The egg shattered, its contents spilling out in a viscous, dark liquid. She moved to the next, and the next, each strike a step closer to the end of this nightmare.

The Sundered followed her lead, driving their blades through the eggs with grim determination. Hikari stood watch, using her flames to burn more eggs as they worked in sections. The cavern echoed with the sound of shattering shells and the heavy breaths of the Sundered.

When the last egg had been destroyed, Kai lowered her sword, her chest heaving with exhaustion. She looked around the cavern, now silent and empty. The weight of what they had done pressed down on her, but she refused to let it crush her. This was necessary. This was the cost of freedom.

Ryn stepped beside her, his face pale. "It's done."

Kai nodded, her eyes lingering on the scorched remains of the nest. "We've destroyed them all."

***

The village of Taepo was a husk of its former self. What once had been a bustling town with vibrant markets and colorful banners was now little more than ash and rubble. The pungent smell of smoke lingered in the air, mingling with the salty tang of the nearby sea. Kai stood in the center of the square, her gaze sweeping over the scene of devastation. Families picked through the wreckage of their homes, searching for anything salvageable. Children clung to their parents, their wide eyes filled with fear and uncertainty.

Hikari shifted behind her, her massive form casting a long shadow over the square. The sight of the golden dragon seemed to bring a mix of emotions from the villagers. Some looked at her with awe and gratitude, others with fear. Kai couldn't blame them. For years, dragons had been a sign that Drakka were nearby.

"We need to start with shelter," Kai said, turning to Ryn who stood at her side. "The villagers won't make it through winter exposed like this."

Ryn nodded, his expression grim. "There's enough wood in the forest to build temporary homes. I'll organize the Sundered to help."

"Thank you."

Ryn gave a curt nod and moved off to gather the others. Kai turned her attention back to the villagers. Taking a deep breath, she stepped onto the remains of what had once been a fountain, raising her voice to address the crowd.

"People of Taepo," she began. "I know you've suffered. I know the scars of the Drakka's attack run deep. But you are not alone. We are here to help you rebuild—not just your homes, but your lives. Together, we will restore what was lost and make it stronger."

The villagers paused in their work, their eyes turning to her. For a moment, there was only silence, and then a man stepped forward, his face lined with age and grief. "And what of the dragon?" he asked, his voice trembling. "Why is it here?"

Kai glanced back at Hikari, who lowered her head slightly, their eyes meeting. She turned back to the man, her voice firm. "Hikari is here to help, just as I am. There is nothing to fear anymore. The Drakka are gone."

The man hesitated, then gave a slow nod. The tension in the air eased, and the villagers returned to their work. Kai stepped down from the fountain, letting out a quiet sigh. Winning hearts was proving to be as difficult as winning battles.

By midday, the square was alive with activity. The Sundered worked alongside the villagers, chopping wood, clearing debris, and erecting the frames of new homes. Kai joined them, rolling up her sleeves to lift beams and hammer nails while Hikari used her massive claws to help clear away larger pieces of rubble. The sight of the dragon working alongside them seemed to soften some of the villagers' fear, though others still kept their eyes on their surroundings.

"This beam goes here," Ryn called out, directing a group of villagers as they hoisted a support beam into place. Kai moved to help stabilize it, her arms straining against the weight. Together, they secured it, and the frame of a new home began to take shape.

"It's coming together," Ryn said, wiping sweat from his brow.

Kai nodded, her gaze drifting to a group of children who watched from the edge of the square. One of them, a boy no older than eight, clutched a tattered stuffed dragon in his hands. He stared at Hikari with a mixture of fascination and fear.

Kai crouched down, beckoning the boy over. He hesitated but eventually took a tentative step forward. "What's your name?" she asked gently.

"Jin," he said, his voice barely above a whisper.

Kai smiled. "Jin, would you like to meet Hikari?"

The boy's eyes widened, and he clutched his toy tighter. "She won't hurt me?"

"No," Kai said firmly. "Hikari would never hurt someone she's sworn to protect."

She extended a hand, and after a moment, Jin took it. Together, they approached Hikari, who lowered her massive head to their level. Kai placed a hand on the dragon's snout, encouraging Jin to do the same. The boy wavered, then reached out, his small hand trembling as it touched the warm, golden scales.

Hikari rumbled softly, a sound that seemed to vibrate through the ground. Jin's face lit up with a smile, and he turned to show his stuffed dragon to Hikari. "See? You look like him!"

Kai chuckled, and for a moment, the weight on her shoulders felt a little lighter. These small moments of connection were what would help heal the wounds left by the war.

By nightfall, the village square had transformed. Several frames for new homes stood tall, and the villagers gathered around a large fire in the center of the square. Kai sat with the Sundered, her body aching from the day's work but her heart full. Hikari lay curled nearby, her scales reflecting the firelight.

Ryn handed Kai a bowl of stew, and she accepted it gratefully. "It's a start," he said, nodding toward the progress they'd made.

Kai nodded. "A start is all we need. The rest will follow."

As the villagers shared stories and laughter around the fire, Kai allowed herself a rare moment of peace. The battle against the Drakka had been won, but the battle to rebuild was only beginning. Still, she couldn't help but feel hope stir within her. They had survived. They were moving forward. And together, they would rise from the ashes.

CHAPTER 17

In the spring, Kai returned to the crumbling ruins of the Tatenagawa temple, her eyes tracing the skeletal remains of the once-majestic pillars and archways. Fragments of ornate tiles crunched beneath her feet as she walked, each step stirring her memories.

It's strange, Kai said. *To be back where it all began.*

In her mind's eye, she saw the faces of those who had fallen: Kokoro, Liu, and countless others. "I won't let your sacrifices be in vain," she vowed, her fists clenching at her sides.

She gazed upon the ruins with renewed hope. Where others might see only destruction, Kai envisioned soaring spires and open courtyards. She could almost hear the laughter of young dragon riders echoing through restored halls.

What do you think, Hikari? Kai asked, turning to the dragon. *Can you see it too?*

Hikari's eyes met Kai's, a low rumble emanating from her chest. The dragon's tail swished, sending a small cascade of rubble tumbling down a nearby mound.

Kai chuckled. *I'll take that as a yes.*

She approached Hikari, her hand instinctively reaching for the Heart of Flame that hung at her waist. The dormant artifact was warm to the touch, a gentle reminder of the power that had once coursed through it.

"We won," Kai whispered, her voice thick with emotion. She stroked Hikari's scales, feeling the strong pulse of their bond.

As the words left her lips, the first rays of dawn crept over the horizon, bathing the ruins in a soft, golden light. Kai and Hikari stood side by side, their silhouettes merging as they gazed at the brightening sky.

In that moment, Kai felt a profound sense of peace settle over her. The road ahead would be long and arduous, but with Hikari by her side and the lessons of their journey etched in her heart, she knew they could face the many challenges that lay ahead.

Are you ready for the real work to begin?

Hikari's answering roar echoed across the land, heralding the dawn of a new era.

THE END

Did you enjoy this book?

If so, you'll probably like my others. You'll find a preview of some of my other works on the following pages.

Thank you for reading this one, and I hope you look forward to the next one!

A Preview of Trial by Sorcery

I marveled at the vastness of the Citadel.

It was home to the Dragon Guard, the greatest warriors of the kingdom. While that was impressive alone, it was made even more amazing because it was also the home of dragons. The massive, powerful creatures were kept in the lower chamber of the castle. At least, that's what my father used to tell me.

A wall forty feet high surrounded the city of Autumnwick, as well as the stone fortress that towered behind it. This was my first time seeing the place, and it was just as large and imposing as I'd always imagined it to be. The massive gates that provided entrance through the wall were manned with guards armed to the teeth. A small line had formed at the entrance as the guards checked everyone entering.

I traveled downhill and joined the line, adjusting my sword belt. The weight of the blade continuously pulled down on my pants. It made me reconsider my decision to use a side sheath instead of one that went over the shoulder. It was too late to change my mind now. I'd spent the last of my coins to reach the Citadel, and I doubted the school would allow me to carry a blade during my training anyway.

The line shuffled forward slowly. I did my best to remain patient, but it was difficult. I was finally here! The home of the Dragon Guard! I'd dreamed of joining their ranks for as long as I could remember. My father's stories had always been filled with awe and wonder as he described his dragon and the bond they shared.

Although it was still early in the day, the sky was clear and the sun beat down mercilessly. I could feel droplets of sweat running down my back and sides. I drank the last of the water in my canteen and continued to wait. After what felt like an eternity of baking in the sun, I was next for inspection. I glanced behind me and saw the line was much longer now. There were at least a hundred people waiting to get into the city.

"Hold it there, low born," one of the guards said.

I looked ahead, thinking he was speaking to me. He wasn't. His attention was on a girl in front of me with long black hair. They'd already given her sack a thorough check, but the one talking grabbed her by the elbow and pulled her aside. I couldn't hear what he was saying to her because he'd lowered his voice, but whatever it was, the girl did not look amused.

"You, stop gawking and get over here."

The other guard was glaring at me. I hurried forward. The guard looked me up and down and frowned.

"What's your business?" he asked.

"I'm here to sign up for the school," I answered, trying to ignore the sweat sliding down my back. The other guard was still speaking with the girl, and he was being a little too touchy in my opinion.

"Another low born seeking fame and riches, huh?"

The guard was wearing a helm, but the ends of his hair sticking out from under it were blond. He was a high born, a noble. They were all the same. They thought they were better than everyone else simply because they were born with a different shade of hair color. I'd been bullied in my hometown a few times, not just for my social standing, and I knew in a city this size that it would be much worse.

The problem with this guard, however, was that he was only paying attention to my hair. He clearly didn't notice the insignia that was sewn into my upper sleeve. I didn't like to flounce it, but sometimes it was fun to bring a noble down a peg or two.

"Stop it," the girl with the other guard shouted. He'd pulled her close and was trying to kiss her. I'd seen enough. I turned my body so that the guard could see my insignia and smiled at him. His eyes widened for a brief moment, then he collected himself and waved me through.

"Apologies," he muttered.

I nodded at him, still smiling, and walked over to where the other guard was harassing the girl.

"Is there a problem, cousin?" I asked.

Both the girl and the guard looked at me. The girl was confused and the guard looked irritated.

"I figured you would have been lost in the market by now," I said to the girl. I was hoping she would catch on to what I was doing and play along. She tilted her head ever so slightly as a wordless sign of thanks and stepped back from the guard.

"I'm fine," she huffed. "This gentleman was just telling me how to get to the school."

"How kind of you, sir," I said, showing off my insignia to him as well. He looked at it, then looked me in the eyes. He hated that he couldn't stop me. I could see the seething anger in his blue eyes.

"Would you mind repeating the directions? My cousin is terrible at remembering things like that. Aren't you, cousin?"

I exchanged glances with the girl. She shrugged. "What can I say? I'm not used to doing things on my own."

The guard glowered at me. Through clenched teeth, he said, "Go straight. Through the market. When you reach the wall, turn right. The entrance is on the left."

Before I could antagonize him further, he stomped past me and returned to his post with the other guard.

"A bit of a jerk, that one," I said. The girl was already through the gate, leaving me talking to myself. I followed her and had to walk twice as fast to catch up.

"I'm Eldwin," I said.

"Go away," the girl replied.

"I'm sorry, I thought I just helped you back there."

The girl stopped and turned around, placing her hands on her hips and giving me a death stare.

"Did I ask for your help?"

"No ..."

"Do I look like some sort of helpless wench that needs rescue?" she demanded.

"Uh, no ..."

"That's because I'm not," she growled. "I can take care of myself."

"Sorry," I said lamely, putting my hands up. Her eyes widened slightly at the sight of my right hand. "I didn't mean to upset you. I just thought … never mind. Forget that I said or did anything."

I walked past her and continued following the road. The girl's response to seeing my mangled hand was the same as everyone else who saw it. Horror, disgust, you name it. It came as no surprise to me anymore.

The buildings on either side were short and squat, all of them built with a dull gray stone. The buildings on the right ended after several feet and opened into a large space filled with vendors. Multicolored tents were arranged in orderly rows and delicious scents filled the air, making my mouth water. My stomach growled and I absently patted it.

My breakfast had been filling, but I'd walked the last few miles to Autumnwick and now I was hungry. Considering I didn't have any money for food, I was hoping the school would provide meals. My father had never told me about his training days, so I wasn't sure what awaited me.

All the sights and smells temporarily distracted my mind from the girl, who I found to be quite pretty. Her attitude, on the other hand, made me question my judgment. I watched the various vendors as they stood under their tents, hawking their wares and trying to negotiate prices with potential customers. The sun seemed to grow hotter by the second as I stood there. I wiped the back of my hand across my forehead and was about to continue to the school when the girl walked up to me.

"I'm sorry," she huffed.

"Don't worry about it," I said.

"No, really. I didn't mean to be rude. It's just …" she trailed off and looked down. "My whole life, people have tried to help me for their own gain. I've made it a point in my life to never need help from anyone."

What she said didn't make any sense. She was a low born like me, so what would anyone have to gain by helping her? I pushed the thought away.

"Apology accepted," I said. "I didn't mean to offend you or anything. I thought that guard was being a little forceful for his own good and thought I could help diffuse the situation."

"Thank you," she said. She paused a moment, then said, "I'm Maren."

Maren. That was different … but beautiful.

"Nice to meet you, Maren," I said. "Are you really going to the school?"

"I am," Maren confirmed. "I want to be a Dragon Guard."

"So do I," I said. "My father was one."

"Was?"

"He died," I answered. "In a big battle ten years ago."

Maren's eyed widened. "Wait. Your father was Matthias Baines?"

I nodded. "That's how I got this," I pointed to the insignia on my sleeve. "Noble by Deed."

She stared at the patch intently for a moment, then turned toward the market. "Something smells good," she said. "Want to help me find what it is?"

I wanted to say yes, but because I didn't have any money, I was forced to decline. Thankfully, she didn't ask for a reason. I wouldn't have lied to her if she had, but I would have been embarrassed. My father's heroics may have earned my family a noble title, but that title didn't come with riches.

"I'll see you at the school," I said.

Maren shrugged and disappeared into the crowded marketplace. A droplet of sweat threatened to drip into my eye and I wiped it away, then continued toward the Citadel.

Girls were odd creatures.

A Preview of Scale of the Dragon

The sun glared overhead, reminding Mina why she dreaded Lord Klodian's summer hunting trips. He was almost obsessive in his desire to hunt dragons for sport, and he used Mina like a hound to sniff them out.

Her life hadn't always been so exciting. Once, she'd been a normal girl that worked the farm with her family … until they sold her to Lord Klodian. Those days seemed so long ago now. At least the memories no longer brought her to tears. She'd cried enough to last her the rest of her life, as far as she was concerned.

"Which way, girl?"

Mina's pace had slowed, prompting Lord Klodian's demand. She looked over her shoulder at him. He sat astride his black warhorse, his polished plate armor glinting in the sunlight. The visor of his helm was up, and he glared at her impatiently.

To his right rode a group of his retainers, and on his left was Vhan, Klodian's squire. The retainers stared at her with a bored expression plastered on their faces, but Vhan looked excited. The squire was always thrilled when it came to dragon hunts.

"This way," Mina replied.

She continued trudging along the dunes, following the subtle pull she felt from the scale embedded in her leg. It infuriated her that Klodian forced her to walk while he and his entourage got to ride horses. Certainly, he knew it would be quicker if she were mounted, but then again, he probably did it just to spite her.

Mina was Klodian's slave, and she knew it. Whether or not it was legal was another issue, but from what Mina had gathered so far in her young life, Dominion Lords did whatever pleased them so long as it didn't get them into trouble with the High Prince.

She supposed it was a small blessing to belong to Klodian. There were rumors that other Dominion Lords could be very abusive, violent even. While Klodian had never raised a hand toward her, he was manipulative and impetuous. Growing up amidst the wealthy and elite seemed to breed those qualities into people, though.

Ahead, Mina spotted a tall mesa that rose several hundred feet above the surrounding landscape. The top was flat, and the sides were steep and straight as if some underground creature had pushed it directly up out of the ground. The rock formation was various shades of red all intermingled, but that wasn't what caught Mina's attention.

It was the shadowed cave entrance.

She angled her steps toward the mountain and the scale in her leg began to burn. It was only slightly uncomfortable, but once they got within a few hundred feet of the dragon, the pain would be excruciating. It happened every time, but that never stopped her. It wasn't the fear that Klodian would punish her that kept her from turning away. It was her hatred for dragons.

They were the source of her misery. Or rather, one of them was. That didn't matter to Mina. The only good dragon was a dead one, and so she would continue to lead Lord Klodian on his hunts with the hope that—one day—he would kill the beast whose scale made her life a nightmare.

"It's there," Mina said. "Inside the cave."

"You're certain?" Klodian asked. "It's not on top, preparing to swoop down on us?"

She turned to regard him. Klodian hadn't kept his title as Dominion Lord for no reason. He'd been born to the position, certainly, but that didn't guarantee someone the title for life. There was always some young upstart who wanted the power and fame for themselves, and Klodian's quick wits and suspicion had saved him from many assassination attempts.

"I'm certain, my Lord. The scale may be a curse, but it never lies."

"One man's curse is another man's godsend. You may not like your ability, girl, but your gift has increased my wealth fourfold."

That was another thing that bothered Mina. Lord Klodian always referred to her as 'girl' and never by her actual name. She supposed he did that out of spite, as well.

"You are entitled to your opinion, as am I. And I say it is a curse."

Klodian laughed and slid off his mount, landing with a clatter as his plate mail jounced about. He unsheathed his sword from his waistbelt and quickly looked it over, then returned it. He motioned to Vhan, and the squire also dismounted. Vhan carried a spear, but the weapon wasn't his. He hadn't earned the privilege of learning to fight yet.

"Wait for me out here," Klodian ordered, taking the spear from Vhan. "I'll be back shortly."

Mina watched him disappear inside the cave. The retainers began talking amongst themselves, sharing gossip and discussing things that made Mina wish a dragon would swoop down on them. Whether it ate them or her didn't matter, so long as it put her out of her misery.

Vhan slowly sidled around to where Mina stood, a grin on his face.

"Don't even ask," Mina said.

"I've never seen it," Vhan replied. "And I *really* want to see it."

"Why? So you can make fun of me, too? No, thank you."

"I wouldn't make fun of you. I think having a dragon scale in your leg is neat. I'd have one if I could. How did you get that, anyway?"

"I'm sure you've heard the stories," Mina said.

"I've heard rumors, which is usually far from the truth. And I've never heard the story from you, so ..."

Vhan stared at her expectantly.

"I fell on it."

"Care to elaborate?"

Mina heaved a sigh, knowing Vhan would irritate her until she gave in.

"I was playing in the hills when I was young, and a hole opened up beneath me. I fell into a dragon's nest and landed on a pile of scales. This one," Mina slapped her thigh, "happened to penetrate my skin."

Vhan's eyes were wide. "Seriously? That must have been amazing. Being in a dragon's nest, I mean."

"The nest was abandoned. And it wasn't amazing at all. It ruined my life."

"You're alive, aren't you?" Vhan asked.

"I exist, but I wouldn't exactly call being a slave to Klodian living."

"Some people don't like him, but I do. He's always nice to me. I have a warm bed and food to eat, so I can't complain. There wasn't much to go around at my home, so being the squire to Lord Klodian has been the best thing that's happened to me."

Mina offered him a fake smile in the hopes that he'd get the hint and stop talking, but he kept yammering on about how great it was to be part of Klodian's Dominion. Mina tuned his voice out and watched the cave entrance, wondering how long it would take Klodian to kill the dragon. Her leg was still burning, which meant it wasn't dead yet. At least he hadn't forced them to go into the cave with him.

After a while, Vhan left her alone and wandered over to listen to the retainers. Mina rubbed her leg, massaging the skin around the edges of the scale. She didn't fear for Klodian's safety. If he died, then she'd have an opportunity to escape. It wasn't likely he'd be killed, though. Not when he had the power of his runes. That was another perk the wealthy nobles enjoyed: magic.

Rune magic was sanctioned by the High Prince, and it was only lawful for nobles to employ it. Everything else was outlawed, but that didn't stop people from practicing it in secret. Although Mina had never met any illegal sorcerers, she knew they were out there. It was whispered that on the fringes of the Dominions, there were people who openly sold their services to others.

The burning in Mina's leg ceased abruptly, and she smiled. Another dragon was dead. *Good riddance,* she thought. A moment later, Lord Klodian stepped out from the cave. He was covered in dust and blood, and he carried a severed horn in one hand. Vhan rushed over and fawned over him, ever the loyal squire. Mina found the display annoying and turned her gaze away, looking up at the mesa's jagged walls.

"That's the first dragon of the season," Vhan said.

"The first of many," Klodian replied. "Girl."

Mina looked at him, and he tossed the horn to her. She caught it and turned it over, examining it. It was small, and she guessed the dragon must have been an adolescent.

"For your collection," Klodian said.

"Thank you, my Lord."

"Ride back to the castle and summon the workers," Klodian instructed Vhan. "Tell them to bring plenty of wagons. The beast was hoarding enough trinkets to fund an army."

"Right away, sir."

Vhan got on his horse and rode off. The retainers gathered around Klodian and listened to him relay how he killed the dragon. Mina ran her fingers along the horn, feeling the coarse lines that grooved its surface. Every horn was different, but they all had similarities. She glanced at the cave and thought she saw glowing eyes staring back at her from the shadows. She blinked a few times and squinted, but there was nothing there.

It was probably her imagination. She waited for Klodian to finish bragging about his kill, and then they began the trek back to the castle. Mina clutched the horn in her hands, hoping that the next dragon to be killed would be the one to set her free.

How she hated dragons.

When rumors of a dragon attack reached Demetrius, he dismissed them almost immediately. Having lived in the port city of Radda his entire life, he had heard many wild stories from countless travelers. Everything ranging from giant squids in the open seas to horses with wings. Admittedly this *was* the first time he heard mention of a dragon, supposed giant mythical creatures that fed on the fear of people and could lay waste to entire cities.

"Rubbish," he said. "Children's tales told by parents to scare little ones into obedience."

"I believe it," the old sailor remarked enthusiastically. "Captain heard it 'imself. Says the whole city was burned to the ground and everyone killed."

"Then how did your captain hear of it?" Demetrius eyed his friend sternly. The man's face was covered in wrinkles and his hair bleached from constant sun. The man had been a sailor since he was not more than a boy and was prone to believe almost anything.

"What d'ya mean?" the sailor, Bannigan, asked.

"If everyone was killed, how did your captain hear this story? Who would have repeated it to him?"

The old man remained silent for a moment and scratched his prickly-haired chin. "It not be my place to question the Captain, silversmith."

Demetrius laughed heartily. "Nice cover up."

The sailor stomped his foot indignantly. "It ain't no cover up. I trust the Captain's word. How's business?" Bannigan changed the subject.

"Profitable, as always. The war with Oakvalor hasn't put a pinch in anyone's pockets yet. I hear some of my fellow smiths have been requested to appear before the king, as to why is anyone's guess."

"Maybe the king needs more weapons."

Demetrius shrugged his large shoulders. He wasn't in the business of making weapons, so it mattered little to him. His craft was typically sought after by the well-to-do, custom pieces that didn't come cheap. Some people had so much money they apparently didn't know what to do with it. He could work with any metal he put his hands on, but he preferred silver. It was very easy to bend and could be cast or hammered which allowed him to form almost anything with it; from teapots to statues.

The clanging of the bell tower echoed loudly across the city, signaling noon. The bell tower was originally built to alert the populace of emergencies. Its main use now was to indicate the time. Bannigan clapped Demetrius on the shoulder and bid him farewell. "That's my call," he said, trying to be heard over the noise. Demetrius' shop was situated near the docks for convenience and the daily clanging of the bell had eventually become a normal sound to him.

"Be safe," he called out as the old man left. Bannigan waved to acknowledge he heard him. Not that anyone couldn't.

Demetrius was a large man with a thunderous voice. At six and a half feet tall, he was a beast of a man, with muscles so large that he had to be custom fitted for his clothing. His hair was light brown and cut short to keep it out of his eyes, and to keep it from being singed. His skin was a deep bronze color as he preferred to be in the sun most of his time.

He watched his friend until he could no longer see him among the crowd. He heard his name a few stalls down and glanced to see who said it. He could see a member of the king's guard talking to one of the vendors. The vendor pointed towards where he was standing. What in the Divines would a soldier of the crown want with him? He watched the soldier approach.

"Demetrius?"

The big man eyed the soldier warily. "Yes?"

"The silversmith?" he asked with an air of impatience.

"Yes."

The soldier withdrew a scroll from his belt and handed it to Demetrius. "What's this?" he questioned. The soldier shook his head. "Not my business, sir. I am just the messenger. I believe His Highness requests your presence at the palace."

"What for?" Demetrius probed.

"Not my business." The soldier's impatience was evident by his short, almost rude, answers. "I must be on my way, sir." The soldier turned and headed back from the way he came. Demetrius stared at the scroll, unsure if he even wanted to open it. Everyone knew he didn't make weapons. Why would the king summon him if he was seeking smiths to make his armies more weapons?

He snapped the seal in half and opened the scroll. It read:

To Demetrius the silversmith,

Greetings from the Esteemed Ruler of Talvaard, King Garun. Your presence is requested at the palace. Do not worry about your business. You will be well compensated. A carriage has been arranged to meet you outside the city of Radda at sundown. Do not be late.

King Garun

There was a fancy signature and the crest of the king, a phoenix bursting forth from a pile of ashes, at the bottom of the parchment. Demetrius sighed. He hated politics.

Dusk found him standing near the road at the outskirts of his hometown. He had closed up his shop early much to his disappointment. There was a certain beautiful woman who walked by his stall everyday around the same time, usually carrying fresh bread. He had only noticed her because he caught her staring at him as she passed by one day.

Her look was one of admiration. At least, that's how he took it. She had smiled embarrassedly and blushed. And so Demetrius made it a point in his day to watch her as she walked by and smile at her.

Closing early meant that he missed her.

He was more than slightly frustrated by that, as he had finally worked up his nerve to actually speak to her. His hope was that she would let him get to know her and perhaps they would see where things went from there.

The carriage pulled up suddenly and Demetrius noticed that the sun was just sliding behind the mountains. "Well at least the king is punctual," he muttered beneath his breath. The door to the carriage swung open and a man dressed in plain clothes, probably a servant, stepped out. He motioned to the carriage and bowed low. "If you would, sir."

Demetrius dipped his head in thanks and climbed inside. A quiet whistle escaped his lips. The inside was adorned with all sorts of glittering shapes. He looked closely and recognized most of the precious stones. Diamonds and rubies comprised most of the decorations, but there were also a few sapphires and a couple stones he did not recognize. The fabric that made up the seats was comfortable and smooth to the touch. It was hard to tell whether the material was dark red or brown in the fading light.

Demetrius was impressed. He didn't expect to be brought to the palace in luxury. Granted he was known among the higher ups for his skills in crafting, but he was not of noble birth. And most, if not all of them, seemed to ignore the fact that he was much wealthier than most of them, anyway. The servant did not get back into the carriage, but instead shut the door and climbed into the seat with the driver.

He had a decent amount of time to think as the buggy headed toward Tarvaarin, the city built around the palace. It was a thirty-minute trip to the palace by horse. After what seemed like hours to him, he felt a difference in the road. Instead of bouncing about on the dirt path, the ride smoothed out and he could tell they were now on the stone paved roads of the city.

The carriage came to an abrupt stop and the door swung open. The servant stood there and motioned for Demetrius to come out. He had gotten comfortable and it took him a minute to move. Why did the king want him to come so late in the evening hours, he wondered.

The servant led him through enormously tall double doors and into a massive circular room that was normally filled with nobles and commoners alike, usually bringing petitions and requests to the king or his advisors. The room was empty and their footsteps reverberated off the walls.

Demetrius looked admiringly up at the vaulted ceiling, rising sixty feet above him. Support pillars were spaced every ten feet, outlining the main walkway through the antechamber. "This is huge," he remarked to himself.

"Sir?" the servant looked back at him. Demetrius shook his head and the servant continued his hurried pace. A door in the middle of the far wall was flanked on either side by two giant alabaster statues of winged men standing at attention, their swords drawn and held up before them. Demetrius thought them an odd addition to the room. The walls were covered with portraits of regal looking men, whom he assumed were previous kings, and large brightly colored tapestries depicting scenes of long ago battles.

He began to wonder why he had never made a trip to the palace, if for no other reason than to say he had been there. The servant stopped before the door. "Wait here, sir," he said breathlessly before disappearing through the door. Demetrius looked down at the floor. Stone tiles, painted orange and yellow, ran the length of the entire room, forming a triangular pattern. The tiles outside the three-sided shape were bright red.

He assumed there was some sort of significance to the design, but it was lost on him. Demetrius looked back up and noticed the servant was staring at him. "His Highness will see you now." He held the door open and pointed down a long hallway. "It's the last door on the left at the end of the hall."

The big man nodded his head in thanks and walked to where he was directed. The hallway, large enough to comfortably hold two carriages side by side, was barely adorned at all. A guard stepped out from the shadows and startled him. "I didn't see you," he laughed nervously.

"That would be the point," the guard answered, his face hidden by the hood over his head. He patted Demetrius down for weapons and finding none, opened the door for him to enter. "Go to the center of the room and do not leave the circle."

"Circle? Why not?"

"Just don't."

Demetrius was starting to regret having made the trip. Then again, seeing how guarded the king was, he doubted he would have lived long had he refused to come. He walked to the middle of the room and noticed the circle design in the floor. He assumed that's where he was supposed to stand.

The guard shut the door and Demetrius was enveloped in darkness. He cleared his throat and the sound echoed eerily. Torches flared to life and revealed a large wooden chair with a man seated on it.

"Demetrius," the unknown man greeted. "I don't think we've had the pleasure of meeting before."

Demetrius wasn't sure if it was the king or not. And if it was, should he bow? He didn't answer. The man must have took his lack of response as hesitance. "You can speak freely."

Demetrius felt a little better that he could speak his mind. He wasn't one to bite his tongue. "What is this about? Why am I here? I am a very busy man, and I have lost half a day's time—"

The man in the chair stood up swiftly and Demetrius fell silent. "I can assure you, master smith, that we are all busy. Some busy with tasks more important than others." The man tossed a leather pouch onto the floor in front of him. "Consider this payment for your time."

Demetrius didn't dare move from the circle to see what was inside, heeding the warning the guard had given him.

"Talvaard has a shadow cast over it, master smith. A shadow that threatens to consume us all."

Demetrius assumed the shadow was Oakvalor, the enemy kingdom that Talvaard had been at war with for as long as anyone could remember. "Then I must inform you, sir, that I am not a weapon smith. I make trinkets and items ordered for noble houses. I think you have erred in your selection of men to build your weapons of war."

"Do you think that I am ignorant of those in my kingdom?" the man asked, revealing that he was indeed the king. "I know what you are capable of, Demetrius, and I have not summoned you here to build weapons. At least, not in the sense that you are thinking."

"What do you mean?"

Several other torches lit up, as though by magic, and exposed King Garun in all his splendor. He was shorter than Demetrius by at least a foot. His hair was long and black, pulled back tight into a ponytail. His nose slanted down his face, reminding Demetrius of a bird's beak. His eyes were hazel and set deep in his head. The king was nothing special in terms of attractiveness. What he lacked in looks, however, was made up for in bearing.

His posture and demeanor exhibited a great deal of confidence and his general appearance was enhanced by his garments. His crown gleamed in the torchlight and gave the impression that it was made of silver. Demetrius knew it wasn't crafted of his favorite metal, but was instead made of something much more valuable: white gold.

It had three gems set in the front. A rare black diamond, twenty karats by Demetrius' estimate, in the middle, surrounded on either side by two green serendibite stones. It was a marvelous treasure. The king's shirt was turquoise and had a lustrous, dazzling sheen that only silk could give. His linen pants were a brilliant green color tucked into black leather boots. During the daylight hours, when dealing with matters of state, he would also wear a mantle that extended to the floor, joined at the neck and open down the front, that was emblazoned with the large phoenix crest on the back.

"I'm sure you have heard the rumors?"

"Of dragons, Your Highness?"

"Indeed. I can read the disbelief in your face. I know how you feel, as I too was of the same mind when word first reached me. I can assure you," the king's tone grew somber, "there is no myth to these tales."

Demetrius was dubious. "What in the name of the Divines are you talking about?

Dragons? Winged creatures that fly and breath fire? You can't be serious, Your Highness."

The king's face remained solemn. "Had I not seen the creature for myself, I would be as doubtful as you, Demetrius. Unfortunately," he paused, gave a great sigh, and continued, "it is very real."

Demetrius was still in doubt, but he didn't further voice his suspicion. "What does all this have to do with me?"

"It is said that no one in Talvaard can work silver like you."

Demetrius had certainly earned a strong reputation for himself, but he was down to earth and didn't like to boast. "So I have heard," he replied, shrugging his large shoulders. "You still haven't answered the question."

The king closed the distance between him and Demetrius with a few quick steps. "I cannot reveal the details just yet, as I myself do not have them. All I know is that the skills of a silversmith are required, along with a few other details. Our ally," he used the word frostily, "does not have the privilege of metal smiths. And we lack what they have. So you see, master smith, you would be doing Talvaard a great duty."

"And if I refuse?" Demetrius asked, more out of curiosity than rebelliousness. A job for the king could prove to be very profitable.

Garun eyed him dangerously. "It would not be in your best interest ... but you have a week to consider it."

Demetrius felt goose bumps run up his back under the king's baleful look. "I am loyal to my country, Your Highness. I would never refuse an opportunity to serve the crown."

Garun smiled, the first Demetrius had seen on his face, apparently pleased with the answer. "My servant will escort you out and deliver you back to your home."

"When will you require my services?"

"You will know," the king answered.

A Preview of Throne of Deceit

The Seven Stars inn was busier than normal.

That was good for business, but it also meant that Gwen had been rushing around most of the evening, filling tankards and delivering steaming food. It was warm, uncomfortably so, and Gwen was glad the night was almost over. The air was thick with pipe smoke and boisterous laughter, a rarity these days.

Gwen spotted a man waving his arm, tankard upside down on the table. She heaved a weary sigh and hurried to the table, forcing a smile.

"More ale?" she asked.

"Yes, and keep it flowing," the man replied.

Gwen could tell by the way he slurred his words that he'd probably already had too much, but she nodded and refilled his tankard. The inn would be closing soon, so not much more ale would be "flowing" anyway. Gwen's father had been in the kitchen since opening, fulfilling the endless stream of orders and cursing when he burned himself, which was quite often.

A bard began playing a cheerful song, his fingers flying over the strings of his lute with a practiced ease. Gwen liked the melodies he played, but he was passing through and tonight would be his last performance at the inn. She did another loop of the tables, making sure the patrons were taken care of, then sat behind the bar and listened to the music.

Gwen found the bard handsome. He was young and energetic, his face clean shaven, and his brown hair trimmed short and neat. Her father would never allow her to marry someone with a profession that required constant travel, but she didn't see any problem with admiring the man's attractiveness. Besides that, it was common knowledge that Gwen would take over the Seven Stars once her father retired.

As the bard finished his song, a commotion outside the inn caught Gwen's attention. She looked to the windows, but it was too dark to see anything other than vague shadows. The noise drew the attention of the inn's customers as well, and the people quickly congregated in front of the windows. Those who couldn't squeeze in among the others exited the doors to see things up close.

Gwen heard angry shouting and groaned. Drunken men fist fighting one another wasn't uncommon, especially when the place was busy. She removed her apron and hung it on one of the hooks on the wall, then walked to the door and cracked it open, peering out into the night.

A single man was surrounded by a group of the king's soldiers. Their black leather armor made them blend in with the darkness, but Gwen knew the attire. The soldiers had become a common sight around the inn, and around Dawsbury in general. Rumors of war had been circulating for years, but now there were signs of it. Aside from the presence of the king's men, there were also whispers of dark magic and sightings of dragons.

Gwen didn't know what to think about any of it. She lived a simple life working at the inn, and she wanted it to stay that way. The king could make war on the surrounding kingdoms if he wanted to, so long as Gwen's way of life wasn't impacted. Her attention was jerked back to the present when one of the soldiers kicked the back of the man's legs, knocking him to the ground. The man being harassed scowled and tried to get back up.

"Stay down, dog," one of the soldiers said.

"Yeah," chimed in another. "If you know what's good for you."

Someone bumped into Gwen from behind and she looked over her shoulder to see Tobias, the baker's son.

"What's going on out there?" he asked.

"Some of the soldiers have taken an interest in Garre," Gwen replied. "Garre's angry, but I think he'll keep his temper under control."

"I can't stand those soldiers," Tobias muttered. "They think they can come to our town and do whatever they want just because they wear the king's emblem."

"As long as we stay out of their way, we don't have anything to worry about," Gwen said. "They're just following orders."

Tobias snorted but didn't say anything.

Garre was glaring daggers at the soldiers, but he stayed where he was.

"Good dog," one of the soldiers goaded. "Now lick the dirt off my boots."

"Screw off," Garre spat.

The soldier who'd spoke drew his sword and leveled the tip at Garre's throat. "What was that, dog? Did I tell you to speak?"

Silence fell over everyone in the inn. Gwen watched intently, her heart hammering in her chest with anxiety. "They can't kill someone for no reason," she whispered.

"That's what you'd think, anyway," Tobias said. "When left unchecked, that tyrant's hired hands will do anything, including murdering innocent people."

"Watch your words, boy," one of the patrons said. "You'll bring the king's wrath down on us all."

Gwen watched with bated breath, silently praying that Garre wouldn't be hurt. She wasn't friends with him, but she knew who he was, and they'd never had any issues. Even if they had, Gwen would never wish harm on anyone.

"Get to licking," the soldier demanded, lifting his boot near Garre's face. For a moment, Gwen thought he was going to lick the soldier's boot. Instead, Garre grabbed onto the soldier's leg and pulled, forcing the soldier to fall onto his back.

"Yeah!" Tobias shouted. "Give him what for!"

Gwen had a feeling something terrible was about to happen. The soldier scrambled back onto his feet and kicked Garre in the face. Garre crumbled backward awkwardly, his legs tucked under his body.

"Gods," Gwen said, flinching and looking at Tobias.

"Someone has to do something," Tobias said. "They're going to kill him."

"Don't say that," Gwen replied.

Tobias stared at her, jaw clenched. "No more," he said.

Before Gwen could figure out what he meant, Tobias drew a dagger and pushed past her. He sprinted toward the soldier that had kicked Garre and leaped onto his back, driving the small blade into the soldier's chest.

The world froze.

Gwen's eyes widened in horror and surprise. She screamed, and the world began moving again, but now it was a blur. The other soldiers grabbed Tobias and forced him to the ground, wrenching his dagger away. The soldier he'd attempted to stab was uninjured.

"Some dogs don't understand loyalty," he said, then lifted his sword up threateningly. With a sudden grunt, he staggered forward as Garre pushed him from behind. Another soldier drew his sword and thrust it into Garre's back.

Gwen stepped back from the door, shaken. Garre screamed and fell to the ground, writhing in the dirt. There was confusion among the rest of the soldiers as they glanced at each other with uncertainty. Tobias broke free of the men holding him and sprinted to the left, running down the alley beside the inn.

The apparent leader threw his arms up. "Don't just stand there, get him!"

The others chased after Tobias and Gwen quietly shut the door and returned to the bar. The patrons slowly went back to their tables, but the mood had changed. The bard had stopped playing his music and the conversations became muted.

Gwen wrung her hands together nervously, not knowing what she could do to help Garre. Should she help him? What if he had done something to warrant the interest of the soldiers and she wasn't privy to that knowledge? She started to head around the bar when the kitchen door flung open and Tobias ran in, followed by Boris, Gwen's father.

"What's going on?" Boris demanded.

"I need somewhere to hide," Tobias replied. He looked around the inn, frantic. Gwen thought he looked like a frightened deer, ready to flee at any moment.

Boris looked around the room, noting the patrons, then grabbed onto the edge of the bar. "Help me, will you?"

Tobias grabbed the other end and, together, they heaved the stout wooden structure forward. Gwen was surprised to see a trap door hidden in the floor.

Boris opened the small door and motioned to the darkness within. "Go," he said. "Hurry."

Tobias didn't question the order and hurried down into the hidden space. Boris closed the door and tried to move the bar back into place, but it was too heavy. He looked at Gwen, then changed his mind and turned to the customers.

"Someone give me a hand!"

A few people leaped to their feet to help and, within a few moments, the bar was back in place.

"Father," Gwen said softly, following him into the kitchen. "You never told me about that door."

"Forget that you ever saw it," Boris replied, washing his hands off in a bucket of clean water. He went back to preparing meals as if nothing had happened.

Gwen watched her father work, wondering why his demeanor had changed so suddenly. There was something he wasn't telling her, that much was obvious. There was shouting in the common room and Gwen rushed out of the kitchen. The soldiers had entered the inn and were harassing the customers.

"Gentlemen," Gwen greeted loudly, offering the largest smile she could muster. "Drinks?"

"We're looking for a criminal," one of them said. Gwen turned her attention to him and recognized him as the leader of the group from outside.

"I don't think I've seen anyone shady in here, but I'll help if I can," Gwen said cheerily. She was surprised her voice hadn't cracked.

"This person is an enemy of the king. He's dangerous and we need to remove him from the streets. He's about my height and build, with black hair."

Gwen put a puzzled look on her face and slowly shook her head. "I can't say I've seen anyone like that in here. Would you like a drink while your men ask my customers?"

"I'd love one, but I must refuse. I'm on duty."

"Right. Can't have you out there staggering around on the job." Gwen laughed. The soldier didn't share her mirth. The kitchen door opened as Boris came out, carrying a tray full of food. The soldier jumped, obviously startled, then calmed when he saw there was no threat.

"Evening," Boris greeted as he passed them, delivering the food to a table by the windows.

"If you see anyone matching the description, please report it to the local constabulary. They'll get word to us."

"I will," Gwen replied.

The soldier turned his back to Gwen, and she noticed the uneasiness of the customers. Most were minding their own business, but a few people were staring death at the soldiers. Boris returned to the bar and the lead soldier stopped him.

"Are you the owner?"

"I am," Boris replied, offering a grin. "It's a humble place, but it's served me well."

"It's a dump," the soldier grunted. "I've also heard that it's a den of protection for the king's enemies."

Boris looked pained. "I hope no one questions my devotion to the king," he said. "I've been a staunch supporter all my years."

The soldier stared at Boris intently, then nodded, seeming satisfied.

"Anything?" the soldier asked his men.

"Nothing," someone answered.

"Let's go, then." The lead soldier looked from Boris to Gwen, then headed for the door. His men followed after him and they exited the inn. Gwen sighed in relief and leaned over the bar.

"That was close," she whispered.

There was a pounding noise at the door and Gwen realized that the soldiers were securing it so that no one could leave.

"Father, what's happening? Why did he say we're hiding enemies here?"

Boris suddenly looked older to her. Deep lines spread across his face and there were bags under his eyes.

"There are things I haven't told you because I wanted to keep you safe," Boris replied.

The customers of the inn began to panic and started kicking at the door. A few others picked up chairs and broke some of the windows, but they were greeted with flaming torches that were thrown into the inn. People scattered out of the way, knocking over tables and spilling drinks. Alcohol hit the torches and flames spread across the floor.

"We've got to get out of here!" Gwen shouted.

Boris grabbed her hand and led her through the kitchen to the backdoor, but when he pushed on it, it didn't budge.

"They've blocked us in," Boris said grimly.

"We're broke," Jayde said, casting a baleful glance at Lochlan, the ship's pilot.

"We'll find another job," Gavin replied. He was always defending Loch, and Jayde hated him for it. Perhaps hate was too strong a word. She turned her fiery gaze on Gavin and frowned. Fine, she didn't *hate* him. But it really annoyed her when he stood in the way of Loch taking responsibility for his mistakes.

"You know, we wouldn't have to find another job if Loch could stick to the plan and quit screwing anything that walks on two legs."

"That's not fair, Jayde, and you know it."

Loch stood up from his chair and crossed his arms. Jayde turned to face him, and they engaged in a silent stare-down. Her green eyes bored into his blue ones. Neither one would give in, and eventually, Gavin stepped between them and smiled at Jayde.

"Come on. We both know that Loch is never going to change, so we might as well accept the fact that he's going to screw us out of a few jobs."

"Yeah, literally," Jayde muttered. "I'll be in my bunk."

She stormed off to her personal quarters, wondering for the thousandth time why she continued to put up with Loch's constant stupidity. It was like he didn't use his brain sometimes and let his second head do all the thinking. They were so close to getting a huge payday, and yet again, Loch had ruined it. The lord of a small planet had hired them to clear out a gang that had taken up residence in his city. While the rest of the crew had been doing just that, Loch had snuck away with the lord's daughter.

A servant had caught them and immediately informed her master. If it wasn't for Jayde's quick-thinking and their even quicker escape, the lord would have executed them all. As it was, Jayde wasn't sure that they had gotten away without repercussion. The rear sensors on the ship hadn't detected pursuit, but that didn't mean they were home free just yet.

Jayde entered her personal quarters and shut the door behind her. She stared at her desk, debating on whether or not she should drink a small glass of Erillian wine. It always helped calm her anger. She was fuming. Loch had managed to really screw them over on this job. Their pockets were empty and her ship needed some work, not to mention they hadn't found a high paying job in months.

She sighed and walked over to the window and stared out at the stars. The vast black landscape stretched as far as she could see. The few stars that burned on the fringe of civilization sputtered and glowed dimly.

"Even the stars are dying out here," Jayde muttered aloud.

If they couldn't find a decent gig soon, she would be forced to land on some god-forsaken outpost until she could afford to refuel the ship. When she was young and wished to see the universe, she never thought it would be in a dilapidated ship with a crew of misfits. Hell, she never thought she'd be a mercenary either, but here she was. Captain Jayde Thrin of the *Determination*.

She snorted and turned from the window just as a massive jolt rocked the ship and pitched it roughly to the side. Everything on her desk slid off the smooth polished surface and crashed to the floor. The whole vessel groaned and Jayde thought she could hear an explosion in a distant part of the ship. She staggered into the hall, stepping over fallen items on her way out. The ship jolted again and she had to throw herself bodily against a wall to keep from tumbling to the floor.

The emergency siren blared overhead, followed by Loch calling her to the bridge. If he was calling for her, then there was a serious problem. He might be a worthless womanizer, but he was a damn good pilot. Jayde hurried down the hall to the bridge, barely pausing long enough for the doors to open.

"Blast it, what's going on in here—"

The words died on her lips as she surveyed the scene. Gavin was barely standing. He was holding onto a console, struggling to keep his balance. Loch was feverishly tapping buttons on the ship's control panel and cursing vehemently. The siren continued to blare loudly, and Jayde had all she could take.

"Turn that damn thing off!"

"I'm trying," Loch shouted. "We've been hit by something and our shields are down."

"Great! They haven't finished charging yet?"

"Not quite. They're at sixty percent." Loch tapped the screen with one finger. "Sixty-five," he corrected.

"That'll have to do," Jayde said. "Turn them on."

"Aye, Captain," Loch grunted.

A few seconds later, the ship began to hum as the shields kicked on. Loch managed to straighten the ship and Jayde sat in the chair beside him and checked the rear sensors. Not far behind them, a sleek Inquisitor ship was closing the distance. Jayde ground her teeth in anger and looked at Loch.

"Nice," she muttered. "Real nice."

Loch peered at the screen and his eyes widened in surprise. "To be fair, his daughter came onto me. I hadn't even noticed her until she—"

"I don't care," Jayde interrupted. "What's done is done. But if we survive, you'll be lucky if I don't turn you in to the Convocation and collect on your bounties."

Jayde smirked as Loch immediately stopped arguing with her. His warrants with the Convocation were a sore spot. Normally, Jayde wouldn't use that weapon against him, but she was furious with him for messing up this time. They desperately needed a payday. Now they weren't just broke, they were being hunted down by the local authorities.

"We're getting a communication request," Loch said.

"Put it through," Jayde replied.

She sat up straight in her chair. Loch tapped a button on the console and the large screen that hung awkwardly above the observation deck window flickered to life and the familiar face of Lord Rasking greeted them. Jayde groaned inwardly but put on a face of bravado.

"Lord Rasking," Jayde said.

"Mercenary scum," Rasking replied. "I find it so enjoyable that I found you with your pants down, so to speak. I'll make this easy for you. Let us board you without a fight and we'll kill you and your crew quickly."

Jayde laughed in response. "Come on, Rasking. This is the crew of the *Determination*. We don't do anything easy around here. I'll tell you what. Run with your tail tucked between your legs and I won't blast your hide to dust particles immediately. I'll give you a head start."

Rasking's face scrunched into a snarl. "The only one getting blasted to pieces is going to be you." He turned to someone offscreen and ordered them to fire. The *Determination* shuddered as a barrage of laser cannon fire blasted into the side of the ship. Jayde felt a slight tremor under her boots as the shields took the brunt of the attack. She slammed a fist onto the console, ending the video feed of Rasking's ugly smile.

"Shields down to forty-five percent!" Loch shouted.

"It's time to show this petulant lord who he's messing with," Jayde said. She pressed a button on the screen and leaned forward to speak into the microphone.

"McCready, get to the gunnery bay and return fire with the plasma turrets. I want that ship burnt to a crisp!"

Jayde hoped the old grizzled veteran wasn't asleep or passed out drunk. A few moments later, scattered bolts of light filled the sky and struck the Inquisitor ship head-on. The enemy ship's defenses glowed red under the assault.

Although the *Determination* was a cargo ship, it was equipped with the latest plasma cannons for self-defense. Jayde had learned long ago that space was, for lack of a better phrase, the wild frontier. Pirates roamed the black ocean of space, looting and pillaging anyone they came across.

"Gavin, get down there and assist McCready. If we can't get a hit on their ship, we're going to be in serious trouble."

The ship's navigator sprinted off to obey and Jayde turned her attention to the console. The shields were close to failing and their fuel was running low. She knew they had enough to possibly get them to a recharge outpost, but it wouldn't be very far from their current position. Unless they were able to maim the Inquisitor vessel, it wouldn't be much of an escape.

A second volley of laser blasts left the *Determination* and struck Lord Rasking's ship. McCready's deep laughter came roaring through the comms speaker.

"We're about to have an opening in their defenses," the veteran said. "I'm going to light him up!"

Jayde had a sudden trepidation about possibly injuring Lord Rasking. He was a member of the Convocation, after all. The fact that he had threatened to kill her and her crew, however, gave her the boost she needed to push that fear away.

"Take it when you see it," she ordered.

"Is that the best idea?" Loch asked.

Jayde ignored him. He had some nerve asking a question like that. Why hadn't he asked himself that before gallivanting with Rasking's daughter? *Bastard,* she thought.

"Call the engine room," Jayde said.

Loch did as she requested. There was a short delay, then Klaus's voice crackled through the speaker.

"I've got some issues down here. Can I get back to you?"

There was a noise that sounded like an explosion, followed by some incoherent shouts, then the audio cut off. Jayde glanced at Loch. Her face remained impassive, but she was sure he could see the uncertainty in her eyes. She gave Loch a slight nod to let him know she had everything under control, then turned to look out the window and spotted Raking's vessel turning in an attempt to flee.

"I don't think so," she muttered. "McCready, hit that ship with everything you've got."

A rain of plasma blasts fell onto the Inquisitor ship, causing multiple explosions to erupt along the vessel. Jayde watched with grim satisfaction as Raking's ship lit up with flames. And then it exploded, sending debris flying in every direction. A shower of metal shrapnel struck the Determination's shield and bounced off, floating lazily through space.

The sudden realization that they had just killed a member of the Convocation made Jayde's stomach drop. Loch wouldn't be the only one with warrants now.

"Get us out of here," she ordered Loch. "Now."

"On it," he answered.

Jayde left the chair and headed for the lift. She needed to see what the commotion was in the engine room. It was a welcome distraction from the fear.

"What was I thinking?" she berated herself. "Now Rasking is dead and I'm screwed. We're all screwed."

The lift came to a stop and Jayde could smell smoke. She hurried down the hall and practically leaped down the short stairwell into the engine room. Now she didn't just smell smoke, she saw it. Black clouds were billowing off one of the engines. Klaus stood nearby, spraying foam onto the flames. The ship's mechanic managed to kill the fire, but Jayde could see the damage was done.

"What happened?" she asked.

Klaus whirled to face her. "You scared the hell out of me! Announce yourself next time, will you?"

"Will do," Jayde replied. "Sorry."

Klaus shook his head and set the fire extinguisher down. He tilted his head to either side, stretching his neck muscles.

"Something hit us hard, which caused a load of debris to land on the engine. I tried to remove it, but the weight of it all crushed the casing and broke the engine wall. We're lucky it didn't simply explode and destroy the entire ship."

"That's good news," Jayde said. "Is it fixable?"

"Not with what we've got onboard. We need to stop somewhere. The other engine wasn't damaged, but it's not going to be able to power the entire ship."

"Great. Let me know if anything changes down here."

Klaus grunted in reply and Jayde went back to the lift. Their already bad situation had just gotten worse.

About the Author

Richard Fierce is a dynamic voice in the realm of fantasy, weaving tales that transport readers to worlds beyond imagination. His journey as a wordsmith began in childhood, but it was in 2007 that he took the plunge into the world of publishing. Since then, Richard has enchanted readers with multiple novels and short stories, showcasing his versatility and creativity.

In the year 2000, Richard Fierce earned the esteemed title of Poet of the Year for his captivating poem, "The Darkness." This early recognition hinted at the depth and artistry that would define his future literary endeavors.

Beyond the written word, Richard is a co-founder of the Acworth Book Festival, a significant literary event held in Acworth, Georgia. This initiative reflects his commitment to fostering a vibrant literary community and celebrating the written word.

A resilient spirit, Richard transitioned from a career in retail to the dynamic tech industry, finding new inspiration and challenges in the world of technology when he's not immersed in crafting fantastical tales.

In his personal life, Richard is a family man, navigating the joys and challenges of marriage and parenting. With three step-daughters (pray for him), three grandchildren, a menagerie of four dogs (his beloved huskies!), and a ferret, his home is a lively haven that resembles a bustling zoo.

Richard's enduring love for fantasy was sparked in high school when a friend's mother gifted him a copy of *Dragons of Spring Dawning* by Margaret Weis and Tracy Hickman.

This transformative experience ignited a passion that has since shaped his literary career, inspiring him to create worlds where dragons soar, and adventures unfold. As readers delve into Richard Fierce's works, they embark on thrilling journeys through the fantastical landscapes born of his vivid imagination.